Seventy Times Seven

SANDRA STILES

ISBN 978-1-0980-6427-3 (paperback)
ISBN 978-1-0980-6428-0 (digital)

Christian Faith Publishing, Inc.
832 Park Avenue
Meadville, PA 16335
www.christianfaithpublishing.com

Printed in the United States of America

1

Frankie Bonita slipped into his bedroom and locked the door. He grabbed a pushpin from his bulletin board and set it on the edge of his bed. Frankie rolled up one leg of his shorts, closed his eyes, and pushed the pin into his skin. He sucked in his breath, then repeated the process again and again. With each jab, his body relaxed, and the tension left his body. He hated harming himself but thought it was the only way to relieve his stress. Besides, it wasn't like he was using a razor blade to make cuts. That time in his life was behind him. Most people wouldn't understand why he felt the need to do this to himself. They didn't have to put up with the stress created by Mr. Fugate, a teacher who seemed to take pleasure in humiliating him.

Students bragged he was the teacher who made learning math fun. He created a class based on games and competitions. This year, he and his class were not fun. Math came easy to Frankie, so he wasn't worried about his ability to do the work. What he was concerned about was the way Mr. Fugate targeted the Hispanic boys in the class. These thoughts made Frankie jab himself a few more times. He reached for his hand sanitizer and a tissue. He didn't want infection, and he didn't want his parents to see the blood. This was a quick solution to both issues.

After getting rid of the evidence, Frankie sat at his desk and began his homework. It took him less than an hour to complete it.

He slid his books into his backpack and walked to the kitchen for a snack.

Frankie heard voices coming from his father's office as he passed. He grabbed a glass of milk and a freshly baked cookie and sat on a stool beside his sister.

"Hey, Tanya, who's in Dad's office?"

Tanya took a drink of her milk. "Not sure. I think it's that new preacher, the one Dad was talking about. Remember, he said one was coming for an interview. I hated when Pastor Simon left. I feel even worse his mom is dying from cancer. Hope the new preacher we get is just as good."

Frankie nodded. "I just hope the new one has some kids our age. I liked Pastor Simon and his family, but it would have been nice if his kids had not been toddlers. The office door opened. Several men from the church walked out. Frankie's father came out with a man they had never seen before. The deacons headed for the front door while their father brought the man into the kitchen.

"Frankie, Tanya, I'd like to introduce you to Pastor Wingate. He's agreed to be our new preacher. He'll be moving his family down here in about two weeks. You'll be pleased to know he has a sixteen-year-old son named Jacob."

Frankie stepped forward and shook hands with the preacher. "Welcome. Glad you're going to be our new preacher. I'm looking forward to meeting Jacob. I'm sure we'll be good friends." Tanya smiled and shook hands with him. She and Frankie sat down while their father walked with Mr. Wingate to the door.

He called over his shoulder, "If your mom gets home before I get back, tell her I took Pastor Wingate to the airport and should be back in an hour or two." Frankie heard the door shut before he could answer.

Tanya grabbed Frankie's thigh and squeezed. "Yea, he has a son a year younger than you and a year older than me." She watched Frankie cringe. A worried look crossed her face. "Frankie, please tell me you're not cutting yourself again."

"Naw, I pulled a muscle in my thigh, and you just squeezed the heck out of it. I know you're excited, but please, for the sake of my well-toned body, no more squeezing, smacking, or punching." Frankie smiled and grabbed her around the neck, messing up her hair. "I love you, sis. Thanks for caring so much about me. Don't you ever change."

As Frankie moved from the stool, Tanya saw dark-colored spots on the leg of his shorts. She smiled, pushed Frankie away, and said, "Right, for the sake of your perfect body. You just don't want me to know how mushy your muscles are." Tanya watched with concern as her brother walked out of the room. She was sure he was harming himself again and wondered what he was stressing about. It had been three years since he had finally gotten help for his cutting. That was also when their father eventually joined Alcoholics Anonymous. She knew that things were okay between Frankie and their dad, so she couldn't figure what the stressor was this time. She hoped Frankie would share with her before he took it too far.

2

Jacob paced the living room, running his hand through his hair. "Florida, Dad? You're moving us from Illinois all the way south to Florida? I can't believe you didn't even ask me how I felt about moving! I worked to make the football team, and we're moving in the middle of the season. You couldn't wait?"

Jacob's mother sat forward in her chair, hands clasped, eyes on her husband. "Now, Jacob, don't take that tone with your father."

Jacob's eyes flashed. "Why, Mom, because he's a preacher?"

His father took a step toward him. "No, because I'm your father, and you're acting disrespectful. Now go to your room and start packing. Your mom left boxes for you."

"But Dad."

"No more arguing." His father pointed to the stairs. "Go to your room, now!"

Jacob saw the bulging veins in his father's neck and knew the argument was over. He stomped up the stairs, the sound reverberating throughout the house. He flung his bedroom door open, then slammed it. So what if it made his dad angrier, at least, he felt better. Jacob grabbed his phone and dialed Jesse's number. He hadn't heard from his best friend since he'd returned from camp the day before. His dad had just given his phone back to him this morning. Jacob listened to the unanswered rings. His dad had taken away all technology and, then, sent him to camp. This was punishment because he got caught making out with a girl. If his dad hadn't gone on the ride-along with a deputy from the church, everything would have been fine.

It was so embarrassing. Tia was the first girl he'd ever asked out. He'd had a crush on her for two years. They parked along the riverbank, talking. Jacob leaned in to kiss her. As their lips touched, he heard a tapping on his window. He saw his dad's face and rolled down the window. His dad preached a sermon, right then and there, about their inappropriate behavior. Tia was so scared that she never went out with him again. After it went around school, no girl would go out with him.

Jacob turned off his phone and opened his closet. Inside sat two boxes with his name on each. His mom had labeled one "clothes" and the other "miscellaneous." Jacob opened each dresser drawer and discovered the contents gone. The only thing left on top of his dresser was his Bible. He looked at his two prized possessions hanging on the wall—his grandfather's banjo and his guitar. He'd learned to play the banjo when visiting his grandfather. His father approved his spending time with his grandfather. After learning to play the banjo, he purchased the guitar. He mowed yards one summer to earn enough money to buy it. It was a simple red cedar top guitar. He practiced daily. Playing the guitar was a calm in the storm he called his home life. He removed each instrument off the wall and gently placed them in their cases, leaning them against his dresser. He looked in the box labeled clothes. His mom had already folded and packed his clothes. The only thing left to pack was his books. He moved quickly. If his father came to check on him like he usually did when he was mad, he wanted to have things finished. He was tired of the daily arguments with his dad.

Finished with packing, Jacob lay back on his bed, exhausted. At almost seventeen, they should have treated him as a young adult and invited him into the conversation, even if the outcome would have been the same.

It didn't seem fair his dad only allowed him two boxes. He wondered if he would be allowed to take his bedroom set since his dad had said nothing about furniture. His grandfather had crafted it with love. The bedroom set was the last thing his grandfather had made; a gift to Jacob before he'd hung up his tools for good. Jacob carried a piece of his grandfather as long as he had the bedroom set. He lay back, mentally and physically exhausted, and fell into a disturbed sleep.

Jacob awoke to a beeping sound. Sunlight streamed through his bedroom window. As he looked out, his eyes widened, and his mouth dropped open. His father sat in the cab of the moving truck, backing into their driveway. Jacob threw on his clothes and ran down the stairs.

"Dad, what is this?" he asked as his father slid open the back door of the truck.

"Our moving van, of course."

Jacob stood speechless. Gathering his thoughts, he asked the question he should have asked the night before. "Exactly when are we moving?"

His dad continued to work, pulling out the ramp and blankets. He brushed by Jacob and replied, "We load up and leave by five o'clock this evening. I need you to go back to your room and begin breaking down your bed."

"But, Dad, what about school and my friends?"

His dad looked at him, exasperated. "Jacob, stop acting like a little kid. You'll make new friends. Your mother went to school to get your records. Go back into the house and do as I said." He walked away from Jacob to the boxes sitting in the garage.

Jacob stared at the back of his father, then trudged back to the house. When his dad said they were moving, he figured he meant they would move in a few weeks. He should have asked. Jacob went upstairs to empty his room. He folded his bed linens and placed them into a neat pile on his floor, then broke down his bed. He carried the bed frame to his dad. His dad followed him back to the bedroom to help carry down the dresser. Jacob placed his guitar and banjo, along with his bed linens and pillows, in the trunk of his car. His two boxes went into his back seat. He helped his dad carry box after box from the garage to the truck. How had he not seen this coming? His mom must have packed boxes and moved them to the garage while he was at school or after he'd gone to bed. Since he seldom went into the garage, he hadn't noticed them. He couldn't believe how much room was left in the back of the truck. He couldn't figure out why they needed such a large vehicle since his father had allowed them to take so little.

Jacob's mom returned from the school with his school records in a manila envelope. She asked Jacob to help her with lunch. They would eat dinner on the road. Jacob saw a flatbed tow truck pull onto their street and thought nothing of it. When he went outside to get his dad for lunch, he noticed two disturbing things; the tow truck and his car were both gone. Jacob ran to the moving van, which now sat in the street.

"Dad, why'd you let them take my car? All my things were in it—my guitar, banjo, boxes, and bed linens. Where'd they take it?" His head throbbed as he waited for his dad's answer.

His dad looked at him. "Did you really think I'd get rid of your car without saying anything to you?"

Jacob didn't wait for a reply. "Why wouldn't I think that? You didn't exactly tell me we were moving to Florida, did you?" Jacob's father flinched.

His dad hesitated before answering. "No, I didn't consult you or tell you in advance. I didn't want the argument. I didn't need you sulking for weeks about something you had no control over." His dad unlocked the back of the truck and raised the door again. "There's your car, Jacob. We used the flatbed to load it into the back of the moving truck. We'll pull your mother's car behind the truck on a trailer. If I get too tired, you can drive the truck."

Jacob's dad closed and locked the door. He put his arm around Jacob's shoulder, feeling him stiffen, and said, "Let's eat lunch."

3

Frankie woke up, dreading his first-period math class. Before this year, he'd always loved math.

He showered and dried off. As he stepped into his room, he reached for the pushpin. His hand flinched back when he heard his sister knock on his bedroom door.

"Frankie, Mom's got breakfast ready. She said to hurry up." He heard her walk away and left the pin on the board. He would have to deal with the stress at school the best he could. He dressed and went to the kitchen, kissing his mom as he entered and sat at the table.

"You look tired, Frankie. Were you up late, studying?"

"Yes. Want to do a good job to make you proud." He smiled at his mom, watching her eyes light up.

"I'm always proud of you, Frankie. I'm proud of both of you." She kissed Tanya on the forehead, then gave them their breakfast. They ate in silence.

Frankie took his dishes to the sink. "I'll be leaving in five minutes, Tanya, if you want a ride." He went to his room to gather his things. Outside, Tanya was standing next to his car.

"You may fool Mom, but you can't fool me," Tanya said as Frankie let her in the car. "What's going on, Frankie? You look terrible. I know you didn't sleep well because I heard you pacing in your room. You haven't done that since you had trouble with Dad. So what's going on?"

Frankie backed out of the driveway and drove toward the school. He didn't speak for a few minutes. "Okay, you can't tell Mom. I'm having trouble with my math teacher, Mr. Fugate."

"You're having trouble with math? You've always been so good with math."

Frankie gripped the steering wheel so tight, his knuckles turned white. "No, I'm having trouble with Mr. Fugate." Tanya pulled away from Frankie when he snapped at her. "I'm not the only one having trouble with him. It's like he is targeting all of the Hispanic students. At first, I thought I was the only one. Jose told me at lunch yesterday that Mr. Fugate walked up to him while he was taking a test and drew a big fat zero on it before he had even finished the test. Something is wrong with the dude. He isn't fun anymore. He's just nasty. I'm failing his class."

Tanya turned in her seat. "What? How can you be failing when math is your best subject? Dad is going to kill you."

Frankie pulled into his parking space. "You think I don't know that? What am I supposed to tell him, huh? Sorry, Dad, I'm failing math because my math teacher doesn't like me. Like he'd really believe that." Frankie slammed his hands on the steering wheel. "I don't know what to do. I dread going to his class because every day is worse than the day before." As they walked toward the school, Tanya rubbed Frankie's shoulder. He hugged her, turned, and walked away, his head down.

Tanya walked behind her brother and watched him turn to his class and take a seat in the front. They had five minutes before the tardy bell. Mr. Fugate turned around and sneered at Frankie. Tanya heard him say, "I see you finally decided to join us, Mr. Bonita." She quietly slipped away to her own classroom.

CHAPTER

4

Jacob looked at the sign ahead that announced he was entering Florida. The sun peeked above the horizon. He compared the flat terrain of Florida to the rolling hills of Illinois. He was surprised his dad let him drive through Georgia since there were still some mountainous areas. He understood why his mom didn't want him to drive through the mountains of Tennessee. Some roads looked extremely narrow, and the drop-off edges seemed too close. He saw a rest area ahead and signaled to turn in. His dad sat up, careful not to wake his wife, as Jacob slowed the truck and pulled into a parking spot. "Good morning, Dad. We just crossed the state line into Florida. I needed a bathroom and stretch break." Jacob gently shook his mom awake, knowing she had to be stiff from sitting in the middle the entire time. Jacob climbed out of the truck and went to the other side to help his mom out.

"Jacob, let's not take too long. Let's refresh ourselves, use the bathroom, and get back on the road. We'll find a restaurant to eat a good breakfast and get some coffee before we go on."

Jacob nodded and walked away. He had wanted to ask so many questions about the move as he drove but didn't want to be cooped up in a truck for 1200 miles while arguing with his dad. Jacob was the first to return. After helping his mom up, he slid inside and fastened his seatbelt. His dad got behind the wheel. The truck jarred to life, and once again, they were back on I-75. It was strange to know he still knew nothing about Strawberry Ridge—their destination.

Jacob saw an IHOP sign. "Dad, there's an IHOP in five miles. They have great food, reasonable prices, and we know what they serve. How about we stop there for breakfast? Remember, they have that bottomless pot of coffee."

His dad laughed. "You don't have to lay it on so thick. I agree with you." His dad found the exit and pulled into the IHOP. Once they'd entered the restaurant, Jacob decided it would be safe to ask about their destination. With such a public place, he was sure his dad wouldn't risk an argument. Jacob followed the waitress to a corner booth, his parents behind him. As he slid in and picked up his menu, he thought it best to order first, then ask questions. He couldn't understand why his dad hadn't told him anything about this place. The waitress took their order and returned with coffee.

"So, Dad, tell me about Strawberry Ridge."

"Strawberry Ridge is a small rural town northeast of Sarasota. I'm to be the pastor of their community church. When I was gone two weeks ago, this is where I came. I met some nice people and one family, in particular. The Bonita's family has a son, Frankie, who is a year older than you, and a daughter your age named Tanya. I think you'll like it here, even if I did uproot you and ruin your life."

Jacob's dad laughed and tried to make it sound like a joke. Jacob tried to be a peacemaker, so he smiled and replied, "Good one, Dad." He looked at his mom and noticed a strained smile on her face. It had been there from the minute they'd entered the restaurant. She relaxed a little. He knew his arguments with his dad stressed her out. After all, Jacob and his dad got along well most of the time. He loved both of his parents. What he didn't love was the way his dad treated him like he was always one step away from hell, and it was his responsibility to keep Jacob from that place, no matter what the cost. Didn't his dad realize that his relationship with God was between him and God? Jacob sat back and sipped his coffee. His mother smiled, noticing how much her husband and son were alike. Maybe things would be all right.

CHAPTER

5

Frankie stood at his car, waiting for Tanya. "Hey, sis, feel like going for a short ride before we go home?"

"Can't, Frankie, I've got a major History test tomorrow, and I need to study."

"Fine, I'll drop you off, then. I need a little breathing room to get my head together. I think I'll go to the park for a short walk. Will you cover for me?"

Tanya hated lying to her parents, but she hated seeing her brother in this much distress. "Of course, I will. What time do you think you'll be home from the library?"

Frankie smiled at his little sister. "I'll be home by six o'clock, and yes, I'll stop at the library and check out a book so it won't be a lie." He pulled up in front of their drive and let Tanya out, then sped away. The first stop was at the library to keep his sister in the clear. He grabbed a book recommended by his English teacher and checked it out. It was one he had read before. He drove to a wooded area not far from his house and parked. He walked the short distance toward the river until he came to a cabin with a padlock on the door. He pulled a key from his pocket, unlocked it, and went inside.

Frankie slid out an ice chest hidden underneath a cot along the wall. The ice was almost melted. He would need to replace it soon, along with the beer. He grabbed a bottle from the chest, opened it, and downed half of it. He thought about Mr. Fugate and what had happened in class. Today was Diego's day in the hot seat. He had asked to go to the restroom, and Mr. Fugate told him he had to wait. Mr. Fugate knew Diego had only one kidney. Diego didn't want to be disrespectful and just walk out of the room, but he was desperate. As Diego stood, Mr. Fugate made it known to the class that Diego had wet himself. He embarrassed Diego as he left the room. Frankie felt terrible for sitting there and keeping his mouth shut. He didn't want to be Mr. Fugate's next target.

Frankie finished his beer and drank a second one. He sat in front of the window facing the river and tried to think about his options. If he told his parents what was going on, he knew there was a good chance his dad wouldn't believe him. His mom would always be supportive. He'd have to give that option more thought. If he went to the principal, there was the chance he wouldn't be believed. If he could get a group of other kids to go and back him up, that might work. He would have to think about it some more. Frankie cleaned up his mess and placed it into his car. He drove down the road to a convenience store and threw the bag into the dumpster, went inside, and bought a small bottle of Listerine and a bottle of water. First, he rinsed with the Listerine, then the water. He repeated the process two more times. He threw the Listerine bottle in the dumpster and headed home.

Frankie walked in the front door and saw Tanya on the couch.

"Did you get the book you needed?"

Frankie knew his sister was trying to cover herself. He sat beside her and pulled out the book. "Yes. I'm telling you that you need to read this when I'm done. Have you ever heard of F. Scott Fitzgerald? This is the coolest book. It's called *The Great Gatsby*." Frankie had already read the book the year before in his honors class. Since it was read in class, his parents wouldn't know he'd read it.

Tanya picked up the book. "Didn't they make a movie with Robert Redford in it as Gatsby?"

Frankie smiled at his sister. "Yes. Hey, maybe you can read the book after me, and then, we can rent the movie and watch it. We can compare the two of them."

"Cool." Tanya tossed the book back to her brother. "Better get ready for dinner. Mom's almost got it ready."

Frankie went to his room and brushed his teeth, just to be safe. He didn't need his parents finding out he'd been drinking. That would not be good. He put his books on his desk and pulled out his math. He'd completed most of it in study hall and only had two more problems. He worked them quickly, then went to the dining room.

CHAPTER 6

Jacob stood next to his dad at the final rest stop before their new home. He heard his dad talking to a tow-truck driver. He was making arrangements to have him meet them at their new address. They had to get Jacob's car off of the truck before they could remove the furniture. As soon as they pulled up in front of their house, Jacob jumped from the moving van and backed his mom's car off the carrier. His dad dropped the carrier and turned the truck around to be in position for the tow truck. He had just stepped out of the back when the tow truck arrived. The driver backed up as close as he could and extended the ramps. Jacob's dad decided he would back the car onto the tow truck himself. The whole process took less than ten minutes. After paying the tow-truck driver, he turned the moving truck around to make unloading it easier.

Jacob's mom went into the house and opened all of the windows to air it out, then waited in the kitchen for the boxes to be brought in. Jacob and his dad carried in the boxes and furniture while she would start unpacking. It wasn't that difficult. They had not brought that much with them. After the truck had been unloaded, Jacob's dad told them to wash up. They were going to turn in the moving truck, get lunch, and then, some groceries. Jacob had unloaded his car and parked it along the side of the house. His mom asked him to drive their vehicle and follow the truck. They made their way into a town called Sarasota. After dropping off the rental truck, they asked about places to eat and was told about several Amish restaurants in the area. Jacob's father drove to the closest one.

Jacob was slightly familiar with the Amish and their beliefs. He had been to Goshen and Shipshewana in Indiana. Both of them were Amish towns. It was funny watching them here in Sarasota. They didn't have the traditional horse and buggy he was used to seeing. Most of them were riding two- or three-wheeled bicycles. The Amish still dressed the same as those up north. The women and young girls wore long plain dresses, mostly dark solid colors. They wore some type of bonnet on the back of their head. The men wore pants, button-up shirts, suspenders, and had beards.

They pulled into the restaurant and hunted for a parking space. Jacob decided the restaurant must be good because there was a long line outside the door. Jacob got out and opened his mother's door. The three of them walked to the end of the line.

The smells that greeted them as they stepped inside was almost overwhelming. The people seemed friendly. They were led to a booth and given a menu. Jacob watched the variety of people who entered and left. When his food arrived, he marveled at the portion of food on his plate. He had never seen such generous portions. After eating, the waitress insisted they try one of their famous pies. His dad agreed. After all, how could you resist such mouthwatering desserts? Satisfied and full, they paid their bill and asked for directions to the closest grocery store. After a quick trip to the market, they loaded up their groceries and drove home.

Jacob helped carry in and put away the groceries and, then, went to his room to set up his bed. If he could unpack quickly enough, they might let him explore a little bit. He set up his bed and removed his books from the box. Sitting on the edge of the bed, Jacob tried calling Jesse's number again. He heard a click and someone on the other end of the line.

"Hello, Jesse?" he was met with silence. He tried again. "Hello?" He heard a sniffle. "C'mon Jesse this isn't funny." The line went dead. He quickly dialed again. This time, the voice on the other end answered.

"Hello, Jacob. This is Jesse's mom."

"Oh, hi, Mrs. Conrad. Is Jesse there? I've been trying to reach him since before we left for Florida." The line was silent except for some muffled sobs. "Mrs. Conrad, is everything okay?"

"Oh, Jacob, I'm so sorry, Jesse isn't here," she said.

"Oh, that's okay, Mrs. Conrad. Can you ask him to call me when he gets home?"

Jacob could hear sniffling and coughing. Then, Mrs. Conrad spoke again. "I'm sorry, I can't do that, Jacob. Jesse had an accident two days ago. He rolled his car coming home from the game and wrapped it around a tree. He was killed instantly. I thought your dad told you."

Jacob held his breath. "My dad knew about this, Mrs. Conrad?"

Mrs. Conrad struggled to answer. "Of course, he did, dear. Your dad came over to comfort us and recommend someone to perform the funeral since you were moving. Jesse was so sad when he learned you were moving. It's been tough for us, Jacob, so I can't imagine how you feel. Please, feel free to call and talk to us anytime you want. You were such a good friend to him and just like another son to us. Goodbye, Jacob."

Jacob sat and looked at the phone, his body numb. He and Jesse had been best friends since they were five years old. Now he was gone. A sudden realization hit him. If his dad had not grounded him for talking back, he would have been with Jesse in that car. Maybe he could have done something. Then, again, he might have been killed along with his friend.

The numbness he felt turned into anger. He had just learned that Jesse knew he was moving, and his dad had purposely not told him his friend had died. How could his dad be so calloused and uncaring?

Jacob had to get out of the room—out of the house. He stormed out and headed for the door. His dad yelled lightheartedly to him, "Just where do you think you're going in such a hurry?"

Jacob whirled around. "Like you really care? Afraid I might walk out the door and not come back like Jesse? What would you do, Dad? Would you even tell Mom?"

Jacob's mom walked in from the kitchen. "Would your dad tell me what? Jacob, what's got you so upset? Sit down so we can talk about it. I'm sure your dad can clear things up."

"Really, Mom? Like he cleared everything up before we left? Jesse knew I was moving, but Dad didn't bother telling me."

Jacob's mom stood at the table, unpacking a box. "I'm sure your dad did what he thought was best, even if it wasn't handled very well."

Jacob's voice took on a hysterical tone. "He told my best friend we were moving but didn't tell me. Jesse got killed, and Dad knew about it but didn't tell me. I'm not a child. I deserve some respect, Dad. At this point, I have no respect for you. Right now, I hate you." He could feel himself bordering on hysteria. He needed to get out of the house and away from his dad. He turned to walk away and saw his mother rushing across the carpet toward him.

"Jacob," she sobbed.

Jacob held up his hand to stop his mom. "No, Mom. Not this time. Don't try to hug me and tell me it will all be all right because this isn't like a cut or scrape that you can kiss and make better. This hurt may never go away."

As Jacob turned toward the door, his dad stopped him. "Jacob, I know you're hurting, but you know what the Bible says about hating someone."

"Don't quote your Bible, Dad. I've had enough of your deception and lies for one day. To think I was trying to be the peacemaker today. Why did I even try so hard?"

Jacob never saw his dad swing. His body hit the floor. His dad's face was blood-red, and he looked like a wild animal. His dad grabbed his shirt and jerked him to his feet. "You will never ever speak to me that way again. Do I make myself clear?" Jacob had never seen this side of his dad. He nodded, determined he wouldn't say another word. He'd heard his mother's cry and saw her coming toward him. His dad released him and turned toward his mother, grabbing her arm to stop her. "No, Betsy, you're not going to baby him. You won't talk, cuddle, and love all over him to make him feel better. He's got to learn who the boss is in this family. Me."

Jacob's mom cried out, her arm turning red where his dad had grabbed her. When he saw the mark he'd made, he dropped her arm. His mom retreated to the kitchen like a dog with its tail between its legs. Jacob stood his ground. He didn't want to anger his father any further. He didn't want to move until his dad told him to. He didn't want to risk getting hit again.

"Don't just stare at me, Jacob, say something."

Jacob glared at his father. "May I please go outside to get some fresh air and get myself together?"

Jacob waited for his dad's answer. "Just go. Get out of here. Be back inside before it starts to get dark. There are a lot of creatures down here that we don't have up north, and no, I don't want you injured or hurt. We'll discuss this later when you've calmed down." His father turned and walked away, shoulders drooping.

Jacob didn't wait around. He ran out the door and around the back of the house, walking beneath the trees. A breeze blew over him, cooling the area where he'd been hit. He could see a river at the back of their property. He walked toward the water, then stopped, remembering that Florida had alligators. He searched cautiously looking for any hidden danger. Spying a small dock, Jacob walked toward the end and sat down, folding his legs underneath him. He stared at the water until he felt a warm trickle sliding down his cheek. He felt so confused.

Were the tears for the loss of his childhood friend? Were they there for the damaged relationship with his dad? Were they for his mother? She'd tried to rescue him. For the first time in his life, his dad showed violence. What was happening to him? There was such anger. Jacob's thoughts were interrupted when a startled fish jumped in front of him. What had made it jump? Jacob watched the water and saw a log float to the top, then realized it wasn't a log. He was looking at his first alligator in the wild. Jacob watched fascinated as it floated in front of him without a care in the world. How he would have loved to be that gator floating away.

Jacob slid away from the edge of the dock and stood up. A canoe sat on the beach. He walked toward it. Suddenly, his dad stepped out and called to him, "I don't want you going near the water. There are alligators and water moccasins that could hurt you."

Jacob walked back toward the house, stopping at an orange tree. He picked and peeled an orange, then bit into it, letting the sweet juice run down his chin. He used his shirt to carry the oranges he picked. At the back of the house, he found a spigot and rinsed his hands before he went inside. After cleaning and drying the fruit, Jacob placed it in a decorative bowl on the kitchen counter. He wandered down the hall to his room and sat in front of the built-in bookcase and began to unpack his books. Several of these books had been favorites from his middle-school years. His Max Elliot Anderson books were among those favorites. The Sam Cooper series was passed around to his friends.

When younger, he and his friends took the role of different characters and pretended that they were the ones having the adventures. They would talk for hours about how they would have handled the situations the boys in the book found themselves in. Since he never really went anyplace, this was his only opportunity to have adventures. He could live them out through the books. His favorite Anderson book had been *Barney and the Runaway*. He thought about the time he had run away to his grandma's house after he and his dad had argued. His thoughts, at the time, had been, *I'll show my dad, I'm running away. Then, he'll be sorry*. His grandmother had talked him into going home. His dad met him with the book. They had actually read it together. Even though he and his dad still had problems, he knew his dad loved him. That's what made this situation so confusing and hurtful. How could someone who loved you treat you like this? How could his dad keep secret something so crucial as the death of his best friend?

He found Tim Shoemaker's book, *Back Before Dark*, at the bottom of the stack. The story of an abduction and the friends who didn't give up looking for him. Just holding the book triggered another memory—a real-life kidnapping of a boy he knew from school. At the time, the news story had scared him to his very core. He'd prayed for the boy with his dad that night, and thankfully, the boy had been released, unharmed, the next morning. A true story that ended well.

He looked at the stack of books again. In a way, these books were all a part of his own story. This is where he went when he wanted to escape his problems. He looked through the other books by Andrew Klavan, Jerry B. Jenkins, and Robert Liparulo.

They were his friends just like his music. Jacob looked up and saw his phone on the bed where he had dropped it. He sat on his bed and scrolled through the pictures of him and Jesse. He lay back against the pillows as fresh tears began to flow until he'd cried himself to sleep.

Jacob awoke to a dark, quiet house. The clock showed it was two in the morning. He'd slept through dinner. He stood and walked to his door, listening for any sounds of his father before he stepped out. He didn't want another confrontation. He could hear both of his parents snoring as he slipped past their room. There seemed to be an advantage to having terrazzo floors, as they created no sound. He walked into the kitchen and found the light switch. He fixed a bowl of cereal and sat at the table. He wondered how long he'd feel empty. The loss of his friend had left a big hole. He'd come to accept the fact they had moved to Florida and would not be returning to Illinois any time soon. He had counted on his best friend to talk him through the first couple of weeks. Now how was he going to survive? He finished his cereal and rinsed his bowl, placing it in the sink, then slipped back into his bedroom. On his dresser were a towel and washcloth. At some point that evening, his mom had come in and laid things out for him. It was an act of kindness. He would need to find some way to show his mom how much it meant to him without his dad's knowledge. He had to get his mom to stop babying him. This act alone made his dad more furious.

Jacob grabbed his pajamas, towel, and washcloth and headed for the bathroom. He stepped into the shower to wash the dirt and tension away while visualizing all his negative thoughts going down the drain. He'd been too angry to pray earlier. Now it seemed that prayer was the only answer to his problems. How was God going to help him? He was here because his dad said *God* told them to come to Florida. How was he to know what God was really saying? Was his dad the only one God talked to in the family? Was it because his dad was a preacher? He was sure of one thing; he was tired of being a preacher's kid.

Jacob slid into bed, his mind replaying the events of the afternoon. He was ashamed at how angry he had let himself get, talking to his dad the way he had. He was surprised God hadn't struck him down for what he'd said about the Bible. Jacob felt so alone. In the past, when he felt so tired and confused, he'd call Jesse. If Jesse couldn't help, then, he would bicycle to his grandma's house. She was always able to calm him down. As he drifted off to sleep, he began to dream about his grandma and her garden.

Jacob was a little boy again, about eight or nine years old. He had ridden his bicycle to his grandma's house, tears streaming down his face. He and his father had fought again. Dropping his bike in the front yard, he ran to the back. As he went through the gate, the bell tinkled, alerting his grandma to his presence. She watched him slow down as he got to the rock path. She knew what he was doing. She watched him step on the first stone. He read it aloud, "Breathe." She watched as he closed his eyes and took several deep breaths. He stepped on the next one and read, "Relax." She waited a while longer, then left the window to get the cookies and milk. She knew when he reached the last stone, he would be calm, and they could talk. She carried their snacks on a tray to the back of the garden. He sat on the ground next to the mushroom sculpture his grandfather had made. She sat the plate on the table and took his hand, leading him to his seat. She used a cool cloth to wipe his tear-stained face. She sipped her tea and waited patiently for him to speak first. Jacob took a sip of milk and a bite of his cookie. "Grandma, why is my daddy so mean? Why does he always yell at me and tell me he's only telling me what God wants me to do? Why doesn't God just tell me? I'm sure he wouldn't yell at me."

Jacob's grandmother looked at him lovingly and said what she always said, "It's tough being a preacher's kid, isn't it?"

Jacob nodded his head and nibbled his cookie. He felt better because he knew his grandma understood. His grandpa had been a preacher. But his grandpa wasn't like his daddy. He always asked Jacob what he thought God wanted him to do.

Jacob briefly woke up, feeling the tension slide away. His grandmother had been in heaven for two years, yet he knew she would always be there to comfort him, even if it was just in his heart. He slid into a peaceful sleep, satisfied that tomorrow would be a brand-new day.

7

Jacob awoke to the calming sound of a bird chirping outside his window. He realized there was a benefit to living in the country. There was no significant traffic noise, no kids screaming, and then, another thought came to him. Maybe that's why his dad brought them out that far. No one would know when his dad lost his temper toward his family. Jacob got out of bed, dressed, then walked to the kitchen. There was no sign of his dad, but his mom was sitting at the kitchen table, drinking a cup of coffee, her eyes red and puffy.

Jacob poured himself a cup of coffee and sat across from his mom. "So how are you this morning?"

She looked at him and smiled. "I'm fine. I'm sorry about Jesse. I didn't know your father hadn't told you. I know you're mad that I didn't tell you we were moving. Your father told me about the move five hours before he told you. He said I had to start packing immediately. He even had a group of friends over to help me. He said he'd tell you when you got back from camp. He had the boxes in the garage for several days, and I had no idea. He'd already packed up his office and what few things were in the garage. Then, he told me he was picking the truck up the next morning, and I had to pick up your records. They were waiting for me when I got to school. It seems he had taken care of everything without telling either of us. I didn't get to say goodbye to my friends either, not that I had that many. I don't know what's going on with him. After yesterday, I'm not sure what to think."

Jacob walked around the table and hugged his mom. "Thanks for putting the towel and washcloth on my dresser. I was so mentally wiped out, I guess, I fell asleep." His mom nodded in understanding. "I dreamed about Grandma last night. I was in her garden as a little boy."

Jacob's mom smiled. "Were you walking the stone path?"

Jacob looked surprised. "How did you know? When I was little, and Dad and I had an argument, I'd ride to grandma's house. I'd step on each stone and read it. It always seemed to calm me. Grandma would find me in the back of the garden and have a snack waiting. She was so great at calming me down."

Jacob's mom nodded. "When I was your age, and my dad and I argued, I did the same thing. I don't know how many times I walked that stone path. If your grandma were alive, she would know what I should do."

Jacob looked at his mom. "What do you mean what you should do?"

"Oh, Jacob, I don't know. I don't want to sound like I'm bad-mouthing your dad. I'm just tired of being treated like I'm his servant. Sometimes I feel like those women in the Middle East. I'm not sure why he treats me like I have no common sense. I know I've not been very good at raising you, and I'm sorry."

"What?" Jacob knocked his coffee over. His mom jumped to get a rag. "What are you talking about? You've been a great mom. Sometimes I wish you didn't baby me quite so much because I'm sixteen, after all. You've always done what's best for me. I'm just sorry that I've been such a rebellious son. I can't seem to do anything right. I make Dad mad all the time, and when you try to stick up for me, then, he gets mad at you. It seems all I do is cause trouble. I try to be the way he wants me to be, but he just rubs me the wrong way."

Jacob's mom cleared the table and began washing the dishes. He grabbed a towel and began drying them. "Mom, I didn't really mean it when I said I hated Dad. I was just so hurt that he kept things from me. It's one thing to just up and move me without saying anything.

It's another thing to keep the death of my best friend from me. Why would he do something like that?"

"I didn't know how to tell you about Jesse." Jacob whirled around. How long had his dad been standing there, and what had he heard? His dad poured a cup of coffee and sat at the table. "When Jesse's dad called me, we were at church camp. If I hadn't grounded you and said you could only go to church camp with us, you might have been killed along with him. I felt guilty as I talked to his parents. I was thanking God that you weren't in the car with Jesse. I had to keep things together for the rest of the weekend. I told his parents I would come to see them when we returned. That's where I went after I dropped you and your mother off. I had already called Reverend Browning. He's the new pastor at the church we just left. He agreed to do the funeral. After I had gotten home, I didn't know how to tell you. I planned to tell you the next day after I got the moving truck. I could see how upset you were about the move and just thought it best if we waited until we got down here and I told you. I'm not per-fect. I obviously made a mistake."

Jacob stared at his dad. He wanted to say something to soothe his dad's guilt but couldn't bring himself to do that. With a blank look on his face, he handed his mom the dish towel. "I'm going to drive around and see if I can figure out this little town. I won't be gone long. I'll program the address into my GPS, in case I get lost." He didn't ask permission, and he didn't look at his dad. He kissed his mom's cheek as he headed out the door. His father hung his head in defeat as Jacob brushed past. He knew his dad felt terrible, but he wasn't ready to cut him any slack.

Jacob drove until he came to the interstate. Seeing the sign for Sarasota, he turned that direction. Sarasota had to have more than the one little Amish restaurant where they had eaten. He drove until he saw an exit sign advertising the John and Mabel Ringling Museum. He took the exit and drove to the entrance of the museum. He parked his car and entered to ask for information about the museum. He would visit another time, but he wanted to take the information back with him. The person behind the counter directed him to an information center that would have brochures about many of the attractions in the area. Jacob collected as many pamphlets as he could, then drove home. He arrived to find his parents' car gone and his mother in the living room with her laptop.

Jacob's mom motioned for him to sit beside her on the couch. "Jacob, I thought about your dream. We could create our own little garden here with our own little stones. I've already talked with your dad, and he gave me permission, as long as I don't spend too much money on the stones." She smiled with excitement. "What if we go to the craft store and get one of those molds and pour our own cement stones. We can put little jewels on them and paint them with our own messages. Then, all we have to do is seal them with some sort of sealer. Do you think you could help me do that?"

For the first time since the move, Jacob felt a sense of home. "Sure, Mom. If you get the sayings for the stone, I can pour, paint, and seal them. I think we need to go outside and plan it out. Let me get a notebook." His mom's eyes sparkled. Jacob met his mom outside and followed her to the back of the house. A swing sat off to the left side of the yard. How had he not seen that when he had been out there before?

His mom walked to the swing and sat down, motioning him to do the same. "I thought maybe we could design a path that led from the back door of the Florida room to this swing. The Jefferson's lived here before us and left this yard swing. We can line each side of the stones with plants. I'll have to go to one of those home stores with a garden department and find out what would work best. They always have clearance plants. Maybe we can find a couple of small chairs and a table to sit out here in the shade. I'm sure there are some thrift stores around."

Jacob could see how excited his mom was getting. She was in her element when it came to gardening. Their garden back home was beautiful. It made him happy to see her like this. It was times like this that he felt close to her. He leaned over and gave her a quick hug and kiss on the cheek, then handed her the sketch he'd made and went inside. His father was just coming in the front door as Jacob entered the Florida room.

"Jacob, I need you to come into the office. We need to talk about Sunday." Jacob dreaded the first Sunday in a new church. His dad always required the family to join him at the pulpit. Jacob's mom would talk about the groups she would start for the women. Jacob would be expected to talk about the benefits of being a Christian teen. It was just one more way of getting teens to avoid him. His dad didn't understand.

Jacob entered the office and sat in a chair across from his dad's desk with its opened Bible and notepad. He must have been working on his Sunday sermon. "Things are going to be a little different this Sunday. In the past, I've brought both you and your mother on stage to stand beside me. This year, I'm going to ask you and your mother to sit in the front pew, and when I call you, I want you to stand so that I can introduce the two of you to the church, and then, you may sit back down."

Jacob breathed a sigh of relief. "Thanks, Dad. I always felt awkward standing up there, talking. I didn't know anyone, and they looked at me like I had two heads. It was a real friendship killer. Besides, that's what you get paid to do." He chuckled.

"Well, glad to know how you've always felt. Since we've been here only a few days, I thought it better if you and your mother talked to your Sunday School classes instead of the entire congregation." The color drained from Jacob's face. "I met with the board last night, and we all agreed that since this is such a small church, it would be best if you talked about what it is like to be a Christian teen in today's wicked world." Jacob stared at his dad. "I've taken down some notes and scriptures for you. It should help. Just follow my outline."

Jacob stood up from the chair and paced around the room. "But Dad, I don't want to teach anything to my class. I don't know any of them. You're the preacher."

"You won't be speaking to your class." Jacob looked confused. "You'll be speaking to the entire youth department." His dad might as well have punched him in the gut. He wanted to vomit.

"Dad, I can't," he said.

The color began to rise in his dad's face. "Yes, you can, Jacob, and you will. There won't be any more arguing. I've spoken my piece." He reached for the notepad and tore off several sheets. "I want you to go your room and study these notes. Tonight, at dinner, we'll discuss what you and your mom will be saying at church."

Jacob looked at his dad. "You're kidding, right? Don't tell me that you wrote a speech for Mom too." Jacob knew he was on treacherous ground, but he continued anyway. "What's wrong, Dad, aren't Mom and I good-enough Christians? Are you afraid we will embarrass you by not saying the right thing?" Jacob saw his dad rise from his chair, bringing the notes around the desk. Jacob tried to stop his mouth, but he just kept going. "What happened, Dad, the church back home got too big for you to see your own handiwork in everyone and everything? Can't trust us to be good, responsible little Christians?" Jacob knew he was disrespectful but couldn't seem to shut his mouth.

The slap seemed to come from nowhere. The force of it threw Jacob to the floor. This was the second time in two days his dad had struck him. He scrambled backward out the door before his dad could say anything else.

Jacob's father sat and threw the notes on the desk, putting his head in his hands. What was wrong with him? He'd never raised a hand to anyone in his family. He'd always been able to keep that hidden side of himself under control. Many times, he had been tempted to lash out with physical force. But he had to remind himself he was a preacher, and it wouldn't look good if his congregation found out he had no control of his own family or himself.

Jacob sat in the small boat on the bank of the river, listening to the water slapping against the end of the canoe, and looked around. He had wanted to hate this place, thinking that this must be hillbilly territory. A gentle breeze blew across the river. The weather would be milder in the fall, but it was nothing like up north. The temperatures here were still in the eighties. He looked down where he sat and thought how mad his dad would be if he caught him in the boat. It was his dad's decision to move them to Florida, yet his dad was terrified of the alligators and snakes. As far as he knew, his dad had seen neither one.

Jacob found watching alligators very interesting. He'd always thought they were dark-green but was surprised to see they came in a variety of colors. The distant bellow of a male alligator and the fish jumping in the river intrigued him. Bugs buzzed all around him as he stepped out of the boat and headed back to the house. Spanish moss hanging from the branches gave the trees a haunted look as it swayed in the small breeze that came and went. The grass, baked dry by the sun, crunched under his feet, reminding him of the sound of walking on snow up north. One thing he missed was the feel of real grass. Most of what he walked on here felt like vines tightly woven into a matted covering, waiting to trip him.

He could smell rain in the air. It would probably be just enough to raise the humidity and stir up the abundance of bugs found here. Jacob heard a rattle as he walked toward the house. He froze in place. The sound was often described as sounding like a baby's rattle, but to Jacob, it was more like sandpaper rubbing against itself. It would be stupid to move without knowing exactly where the snake was. He looked around and saw it off to his left, lying in a patch of sun, trying to collect as much warmth as it could before it got too hot. Jacob took two steps backward and moved to the right, grabbing an orange from the tree. He sat in the swing while he ate the fruit. Jacob dreaded going back into the house and the confrontation that was coming. If he could, he would sit and eat while listening to his dad. Besides, there was nothing to say. He could no longer trust himself to keep the peace between himself and his dad.

Jacob walked into the kitchen and washed his hands, then helped his mom set the table while she served up the food. They sat together, bowing their heads as his dad said the blessing. He glanced at his mom and saw a strained look on her face. She refused to look at Jacob. He spoke first to break the tension. "The roast tastes great, Mom."

She didn't reply. "The potatoes and carrots have a great texture to them."

His mom dropped her fork. Her lips began to tremble. "Oh, for heaven's sake, Betsy, stop your blubbering around," said his dad. "Can't we just have one normal meal? Does everything have to contain drama?" Betsy continued to stare at her plate.

Jacob looked from his dad to his mom. "I'm sorry if I upset you, Mom, I didn't mean anything by it." Jacob's dad slammed his fork down.

"You didn't upset her. I did. I told her she needed to stop treating you so special. Maybe if she'd done as I'd instructed her years ago, you wouldn't be such a rebellious child. It's time your mom figured out her place in this family and stayed there." Jacob saw tears forming in his mother's eyes. "Don't bother saying anything to her. I've told her she's to keep her mouth shut, unless I tell her to open it. I'm in charge here. God made me the head of this house, and it's time the two of you got with the program. The Bible says a wife is to be in submission to her husband. What I say goes. Things will go smoothly as long as both of you remember your place."

Jacob stared at his dad. This was unbelievable. Jacob's mom slowly stood and looked at her husband. "I would like to ask permission to leave the table, please." His dad looked at her and shook his head.

"No. We're not finished eating, Betsy. No one leaves the table until you've eaten like all normal families. No more garbage today." His mom sat back down and picked up the fork. She stabbed a potato and put it in her mouth as the tears slid silently down her cheeks. Jacob smashed his carrots and potatoes down, layering the potatoes, carrots, and meat on his bread, then folded it in half. He bit off a large chunk and tried to chew it. He found this a difficult task as his mouth seemed to be extra dry. Jacob's father finished first. He sat with his arms folded and watched them until they had cleaned their plates. "You may clean up the dishes now, Betsy. Jacob, go take your shower and start studying. I put the notes on your bed. We'll get up an hour early tomorrow morning so you both can practice on me." With that, his dad left the room.

Jacob started to open his mouth. His mom held up her hand and sent him to his room. Jacob walked down the hall, listening to his mom as she slammed the dishes in the dishwasher. He wished he could comfort her but knew his dad would never allow it. He wanted Monday to come so he could start school and be away from his dad.

Frankie woke up, excited to go to church. He wanted to meet the new preacher's son. He hoped they would be friends. Tanya knocked softly on his door. Frankie let out a whistle as he opened the door and looked at his sister. She was really dressed up. Frankie figured she must be hoping to make a good impression on the new kid.

Tanya twirled around. "Well, Frankie, what do you think? Not too dressy, is it?"

Frankie joked, "I don't know, Tanya, I might not be able to fight off all the guys to protect you today. Seriously, sis, you look fabulous." Frankie pretended to be shocked when Tanya hugged him. He would do anything for his sister. He didn't want her to feel out of place, so he chose to wear his suit. Most of the youth didn't wear a suit to church on Sunday. That was one reason he loved his church; it was so informal. Now all he had to hope was that the new kid didn't come in jeans.

Frankie joined his sister and parents at the table. His mom had made sure they had a large breakfast. Evidently, they were going to be at church for quite some time. His parents complimented both of their children on their choice of clothing.

"It's important that we make a great impression on the new preacher's family. I'm proud of you." Frankie's dad looked at each of them. His statement made Frankie uneasy, but he didn't know why. He brushed the thought away and finished his breakfast.

Tanya helped her mother load the dishwasher. "Have you seen the new kid, Mom?"

"No, sweetie, I haven't. I don't even know his name. It's like your dad and new preacher have been keeping everything secret. I'm not sure why that makes me uneasy. I guess it reminds me of the times when he kept secrets from us. We never knew what to expect. But your dad is a different person now, and I can't imagine anything sinister with the new preacher." They finished quickly and went to their rooms to finish preparing.

Tanya heard the horn honking. She and her mother rushed out of their rooms and collided. "Wow, Mom, you look great." Her mom smiled at her daughter. Tanya laughed. "We'd better hurry before Dad decides to drive inside to get us." They rushed down the hall and outside.

Mr. Bonita stood next to the car with a look of displeasure. "You're going to make us late. Maybe the two of you should not have been so vain today." He sat in the car and waited for them to get in. Mrs. Bonita looked at her husband and wondered if her husband was back to his old ways. It had been several years since he talked to his family like he did today. She said a silent prayer and, then, pasted on a smile.

Jacob's alarm went off at 5:30 a.m. His dad must have set it because he would never have set it that early. He got out of bed and noticed his suit on the back of his desk chair. If the other kids didn't dress up, he would stand out even more. He didn't know why his dad insisted that he dress so different from everyone else. In the bathroom mirror, he could see a slight bruise on his cheek. He hoped his dad wouldn't see it. He dressed quickly and entered the kitchen.

Jacob noticed his dad sitting at the table with a cup of coffee. His mom was standing in the middle of the room, speaking. His dad scowled and leaned forward. "For heaven's sake, Betsy, smile." Jacob watched his mom paste a fake smile on her face as she continued her speech. When she finished, she stood still, waiting for permission to sit. "You may sit down, Betsy. Jacob, your turn." Jacob walked to the center of the room and smiled sarcastically at his dad. He talked as fast as he could until he finished the speech. Unlike his mother, Jacob didn't wait for permission to sit. He got a cup of coffee and set it on the table. "Jacob, I want you to do it again. You have all of the words down but not the enthusiasm." Jacob stared back at his father.

"Let me get this straight, Dad. You want me to be enthusiastic about something I don't want to do. I don't think so. When it's time for me to stand before the unknown crowd, be assured I won't make you look bad. I will be the best actor you have ever seen. You can't force someone to do and say something they don't feel. Not even if you tell them they have to because God said so. I believe, based on your sermons, that God gave each of us talents. Yours is to preach. I'll never find out mine until I am long gone from home because you won't let me learn my talents. You want to pick them for me. I suppose whatever you decide you want me to have, God will give it to me because you said so, right?"

Jacob's dad slid his chair back, his fists clenched. Jacob stared him down. "If you're going to hit me again, Dad, you might want to punch the other side so you don't make the bruise you left any darker." His dad stopped, unclenched his fists, turned, and walked out of the kitchen. Jacob laughed silently in relief. He looked at his mom, her back to him, and her shoulders were shaking. He hadn't meant to upset her so much. He walked to her and put his arms around her and was shocked to see his mom was chuckling, her eyes full of tears.

"I was so scared for you. When you stood up to your dad, I was sure he was going to hit you again. When you made that last comment, I had to turn around and grab the table. Your comment sucked all of the air from the room. I was so afraid he would see me laughing. Now sit down, and I'll fix some breakfast. When it's done, I'll let you call your dad back."

They ate in silence, each loading their own dishes into the dishwasher. Jacob went to his room and grabbed his Bible, joining his mom at the door. The sound of the car starting forced them out the door. The ride to the church was a peaceful time of contemplation. Jacob wondered about his place in the family and the new church. After his talk, would anyone want to be his friend? How many kids were there? Did it even have a youth group?

Jacob looked at his new church as they pulled into the parking lot and realized they were the first ones. The building was white stucco with a big cross on the front. A long building attached to the back of the church ran off to the left. The outside of the building contained little ornamentation. He assumed the inside would be just as simple. Jacob was surprised when he walked inside. High ceilings, stage lighting, and rows of soft-cushioned chairs filled the interior.

He was surprised to see a drum set and electric piano on stage with the podium. Jacob heard voices as the doors behind him opened.

"You must be the new preacher's son." Jacob turned around. There stood a girl with the biggest smile he'd ever seen. She held out her hand. "Hi, I'm Tanya Bonita. This is my brother, Frankie. My mom and dad are outside, talking with your parents. I understand you're going to talk to the youth department," she said with a smile.

Jacob rolled his eyes. "I guess my dad already told you?"

"You could say that. Your dad and the deacons met at our house the other night," Tanya replied. "Don't worry about it. Everything will be just fine."

Jacob laughed. "You can say that because you don't have to stand up there and talk in front of everyone. How many people are in the youth department?"

"Well, you are talking to one-eighth of them. There are only sixteen of us. You've increased our department to seventeen. Now if they bring in the middle-school kids, that will bring the total up to twenty if everyone shows up." Tanya laughed when she saw the look of relief on his face. "Do you really hate talking to people that much?"

Jacob chuckled. "Not really. I just hate finding out about it a few hours before I have to speak. I don't know anyone here yet. The last thing I want them thinking is that I'm some kind of an idiot. I'd like to make friends here."

Frankie looked puzzled. "Why wouldn't you make friends here?"

Jacob looked surprised. "Are you kidding me? Most people find out I'm a PK, and they want nothing to do with me. No one wants to hang out with someone whose dad is going to watch and comment on everything they say or do. Back home, if I wanted to hang out with friends, I had to go to their house. They didn't feel comfortable in my house."

Tanya put her arm through Jacobs's arm. "Well, you won't find it that way here. Let's go meet the rest of the kids." Jacob smiled and walked back outside with Tanya and Frankie.

The church service had gone fine, and Jacob managed to get through his speech. Thanks to Tanya's prompting, the youth made sure to tell his dad what an excellent job he'd done. The Bonita family had invited Jacob's family to lunch. Jacob rode with Frankie and Tanya to their house. He was surprised to learn they lived only a couple of miles up the road from him. By the time lunch was over, Frankie and Tanya had arranged to pick him up for his first day of school. Things were going smoother than he figured they would. When they finished lunch, they offered to clear the table while the adults had coffee. After filling the dishwasher, they went out the back door. Jacob was surprised to see they had a pool.

"Why do you have a fence around your pool?" Jacob asked.

Frankie laughed at him. "Duh, can you say gator bait? Even with a fence around the pool, we always check the water before we go in."

Jacob still hadn't figured out what Frankie was talking about. "Check it for what?"

Frankie slapped his hand to his head. "Alligators. They don't usually climb fences to get to the water. However, on occasion, they do. I personally don't want to jump into the pool and become food."

The three of them walked across the backyard toward the river. Frankie figured he'd better teach Jacob a little bit more about alligators. "Don't ever go down to the water's edge at night or when it is getting dusk. Alligators like to hang out under the dock or on the beach. You can shine a light down there, and if there are alligators, you'll see their red eyes glowing. They won't usually bother you if you stay away. You do need to be careful when it's mating season or when there are babies around. The adults are very protective."

"Well, that doesn't sound like anything too hard to follow. I didn't think I'd like it down here. It's so different from where I came from. We lived in a medium-sized town. The church was about twice the size of this and had four times more youth. The funny thing is I had only one good friend at that church. He was the only one that wasn't afraid to come over to my house. My dad just couldn't seem to scare him off. We'd been best friends since we were little." Jacob got really quiet. "It doesn't matter anymore. He got killed in a car accident right before we left."

Frankie was the first one to speak. "Oh man, that's tough. I'm sorry. I know we've just met and all, but I think you're okay for a—what did you call yourself—a PK? What does that mean, anyway?"

Jacob was surprised Frankie had never heard of a PK. "Really? You don't know what PK stands for?" Frankie shook his head. Jacob laughed, and mocking Frankie, he slapped his head and said, "Duh, preacher's kid." Tanya cracked up. Frankie looked dumbfounded, then joined them in their laughter.

10

Jacob woke early Monday morning, hoping to avoid his dad. In the kitchen, he found both of his parents sitting at the table. His mother had a bowl of oatmeal and a glass of juice waiting for him. It was just like his mom to make sure he had everything he needed for a nutritional start to his first day at school. Jacob sat down and said a quick prayer over his food. Before he could take his first bite, his father spoke.

"I don't want you driving to school until you learn the route and until I give you permission. After your behavior yesterday morning, I think that you can just wait another week to drive any place. I spoke with Mr. Bonita yesterday, and he said his son would pick you up this week." His father shook the paper he was hiding behind as if to straighten it out, refusing to look at his son. Jacob simply agreed with his father. He wanted no confrontation before he left for school.

Jacob finished his breakfast. He gathered his things and stood outside to wait for his ride. Frankie pulled into his drive and waved. Tanya slid out of the front seat and into the back.

"Hey, I can sit in the back, you didn't need to move." Tanya smiled and sat back. Jacob slid into the front seat. "Nice car, man."

Frankie smiled with pride. "Hey, thanks. It was a birthday gift from my grandfather last year. It was his 1969 AMX. My dad was furious when he gave it to me. I guess it was supposed to be my dad's car, but something happened, and he didn't give it to him."

Tanya leaned forward in her seat. "I'll show you to the office when we get to school. You can get your schedule there. If you want, I'll wait with you and show you where your first class is. I can point out some of the important places you'll need to know."

Jacob turned and smiled at her. "Hey, I appreciate that. I hate starting new schools. You don't know anyone, and you don't know where you're going. Is it a large school?"

Tanya looked at him through her long eyelashes, hoping to impress him enough he'd ask her out. She shook her head.

"There are only about nine hundred students here. We've managed to keep it small. Every now and then, the school board tries to change the district lines so we have more kids."

Jacob turned in the seat and looked at her. "What stopped them from doing it? Where I come from, the school district did what they wanted."

Frankie joined the conversation. "For one thing, we have a very active parent organization at our school. They aren't afraid to stand up in meetings here at the school and at the school board. The second thing is we're so far out that parents don't want to drive this far to get their kid if they get sick. Right now, there are just a few housing developments in the area, and then, there are those like us who just like living in the boonies."

Frankie made a sharp turn into a parking lot in front of a two-story white building. The columns in front were painted red. "Wow," Jacob said. "Those are some bright colors. What's your mascot here?"

Frankie unbuckled his seatbelt and opened the car door. He turned and looked at Jacob. "Our team is known as the Red Hawks. That would be fine except everywhere you see the logo, the stupid bird has a strawberry in its claws." Frankie pulled his seat forward and grabbed his backpack. Jacob stepped out and helped Tanya pull herself from the tiny space in the back. He hadn't realized how tight it was back there. She thanked him as they walked to the front of the building.

Frankie said goodbye and headed off to find his friends while Tanya walked with Jacob to the office. "Hi, Mrs. Johnson. This is our new student, Jacob Wingate. His mom should have brought his records last week. Do you have a schedule for him?" She waited until Mrs. Johnson found his records and handed Jacob his schedule. Jacob thanked her and walked out of the office. Tanya looked over his shoulder and grinned.

"Okay, Tanya, what's up? Why the grin? Let me guess. I've got the lamest classes, and they put me in the basement of the school." He laughed at his own joke.

Tanya punched his arm. "First, we don't have a basement. This is Florida, remember? Second, I see here that I will be your guide all day long. It seems we have identical schedules."

"No way." Jacob snatched the schedule from her hands. He had no idea what his mom had signed him up for. He had Honors English, Chemistry 1, Algebra 2, Spanish 2, SAT Prep, and Beginning guitar. "No way, no way, no way." He looked at Tanya. "You have guitar classes here?"

"Sure? Did you take lessons at your old school?"

Jacob snorted. "No way. My dad wouldn't let me take lessons because our school didn't have classes for guitar. Everything I know about playing guitar I've learned from watching videos on the internet." Jacob looked very excited. No way his dad could stop this. He would have to thank his mom when he got home. She knew what he would have chosen. If his dad had registered him, he would have picked something that involved business or technology. There was no doubt when he saw Jacob's schedule that he would consider the lessons frivolous.

Tanya watched the mood change in Jacob. His smile had turned into a frown. "Is something wrong with your schedule?" she asked him.

"Not at all, Tanya. I was just thinking about how I could make it up to my mom for putting the guitar class in there. Then, I started thinking about how unhappy my dad is going to be about the guitar class."

Tanya smiled her charming smile and said, "Let me take care of that. I'll come in and talk about the classes we have together when we get to your house and why I'm taking the guitar class. I'm sure he'll be okay with you taking the class after I talk to him."

"So tell me why you're taking the guitar class." Jacob stopped and made Tanya look at him. He waited for an answer. She acted like she was trying to decide whether to tell him or not.

She shook her head and said, "Nope. Not until we get to your house. You'll just have to wait." Jacob grabbed his chest and groaned like he was in pain. "It's going to be agony waiting all day." Tanya laughed at his joke.

Jacob had successfully made it through his classes to lunch. He followed Tanya through the line, paid for his food, then followed her outside to a table. He bowed his head and prayed silently. Tanya did the same. As he lifted his head, he was bumped from behind. "Look at the preacher boy, getting all holy on us." Jacob turned red. He didn't know who the boys were, but it was apparent they had already found out he was a PK. Nothing ever changed about that. Jacob ate his lunch in silence, wanting nothing more than to get out of there. When they finished, he asked Tanya if they could go to the library. They emptied their trash and walked to the library. Tanya introduced him to Mrs. Kelly, the librarian. Jacob browsed the new books Mrs. Kelly had to be filed on the shelves and found one he had not read. Tanya looked over his shoulder, reading the title *The Sect: The Windgate* by Braxton Cosby. She'd never heard of the book or the author. He took it to the front and checked it out. The librarian looked at the book and, then, at him. "Are you sure you want to check this book out? We just got it in, and I'm not sure what it's about. I haven't read it yet."

Jacob looked at her and smiled while he handed her his ID card. "I'm very sure about this. I've read one of his other books. He's quite good. You said you just got the book in and didn't know what it was about. What made you order it?"

Mrs. Kelly handed him his card and the book. "It was donated by a teacher. She said it was excellent and that the students would love it. She reads so many books that if she says it's good, it usually is. She said it's full of adventure, suspense, fighting. You know, all the things you, young kids, like. So why don't you read it and come back and tell me what you think? Maybe I'll read it then."

Jacob laughed. "You got it. I'll report back as soon as I finish it." Tanya was waiting for him near the exit. They walked to their next class together, talking about the books they enjoyed. When school was out, they met Frankie at his car. Frankie pulled into Jacob's drive. Jacob invited them in so Tanya could talk with his dad.

As they stepped from the car, Frankie pointed to a car sitting beside the house. "What in the world is that monstrosity?"

Jacob stood up taller. "That monstrosity as you choose to call it is my car. It's a 1972 Datsun 610. As you can see, it blends in quite nicely with the Florida greenery. So please do not insult my ride. I worked hard for that car." He looked at Frankie as if he was hurt; then, he started laughing.

Frankie bowed with an exaggerated flourish, "Excuse me, I did not mean to offend my new best friend. Please, forgive me." They both cracked up. They entered the house, and Jacob made sure his mom knew he was home and that he'd brought friends with him. They sat in the kitchen, enjoying sodas and talking with his mother about Jacob's first day. Jacob heard his dad's office door open.

"So Jacob, how was the first day of school?" His dad asked as he poured a cup of coffee and joined them at the table. "Did you get your schedule and everything this morning?"

Jacob nodded. He hated feeling like his dad was grilling him for some secret. "The day was great. Tanya and I share all of the same classes. Get this, Dad, our last class of the day is guitar class. Now I don't have to worry about paying for lessons. It's actually one of my courses. Mr. Wagner, the teacher, had me show him how much I knew, and surprisingly, I'm right up there with the rest of the class."

Jacob's father shot a disapproving look at his wife. Before his father could open his mouth, Tanya spoke. There was excitement in her voice. "I think it is so cool that we're taking this together. We have a small youth band at church. Soon, Jacob and I will have learned enough that we can join the other youth in the praise band at church. We'll be able to share our passion and the talent God gave us with the church. I am so excited that I have someone else that loves to praise God with music just like I do."

Jacob's father remained silent, his eyebrows raised. He'd been completely blindsided by this enthusiastic young girl. Her seeming passion for serving the Lord and her church was outstanding. It was wonderful knowing that this type of influence was going to rub off on his son. Maybe there was hope that his son would secure his place in heaven, after all. He smiled at her. "That is wonderful." He excused himself and went back into the office. When the door had shut, Jacob and his mom looked at Tanya.

Jacob's mom smiled and relaxed. "I was so sure when he found out I'd signed you up for a guitar class that he'd be furious. I can't believe what I just saw. I'll leave you young people to talk for a while. Not too long, Jacob. You need to get your homework done."

Jacob let his mom give him a hug and waited until she had left the room. He looked at Frankie and, then, at Tanya. "You are so good, I thought sure he would hit the ceiling. He's never allowed me to take lessons. He said if God wanted me to be able to play, he would have given me the talent."

Frankie looked puzzled. "That makes no sense. I'm sure God gave him a talent for preaching, but he had to take lessons to perfect it, right?"

Jacob laughed. "Good point. May I use that argument the next time he tells me how something I want to learn is unnecessary? His philosophy is that God will give me all the talents I need. I guess that could also mean that I should be able to pass my classes without studying, right?"

Tanya shook her head. She and Frankie stood up and put their empty glasses in the sink. Jacob walked them to the door and waved as they left. Like Jacob, their parents placed great importance on their education. Before dinner was ready, Jacob went to his room to complete his homework. As he passed his dad's office, the door suddenly opened.

His dad stepped out. "I really like that Tanya. She seems like such a godly young lady, so on fire for the Lord. I wouldn't mind seeing you date her or someone like her. Going to your room to do homework?" Jacob nodded. "Great. I'll let you go and see you at dinner." He stepped back into his office, leaving Jacob standing bewildered in the hallway.

CHAPTER

11

Frankie was happy; Jacob had started to pick his sister up for school. He no longer had to wait around for her when she had some meeting after school. This gave him more time for homework and whatever he wanted to do. He'd always been a good student. But he struggled to remember formulas for both chemistry and math. This meant he had to study for tests twice as long as most people. That didn't mean he did poorly in either subject. Frankie left school as soon as the bell rang. He had a math test the next day and needed to study. He stayed in his room and worked until dinner time and, then, went back to work, putting in another two hours. He knew he was prepared for the test.

When Frankie woke, he felt confident in his ability to pass the math test. He was glad the test was first period so he could get it behind him. As he walked into class and sat down, he noticed Mr. Fugate looked extra stressed. He had already snapped at Mario when he walked in as the bell rang. It wasn't Mario's fault the bus was late every day. Then, he had yelled at Jose when his pencils fell to the floor. Frankie had noted a sharpness to Mr. Fugate's voice over the past week. He assumed he was stressing like all the other teachers with the new curriculum guidelines. Frankie began the test the minute he received it. It wasn't long before his mind went blank. He couldn't remember the formulas needed to solve the math problems. He didn't know why Mr. Fugate refused to allow them to use a formula sheet; the other math teachers did. When they took the state test, they were given formula sheets. Mr. Fugate called them "cheat sheets" and said the only reason he handed them out was that he had to follow the testing rules. Frankie lowered his head to the desk and tried to remember the formulas. His head began to throb. That was the problem with stressing over tests; he always ended up with a stress headache. He could feel his heartbeat in his temples and knew that this one was going to be a doozy. As he rubbed his head, he mumbled under his breath. He tried to pull the formulas he had studied so hard the night before from his brain. He did a simple head roll to try to relieve the pressure that was slowly building.

Mr. Fugate had been teaching for eighteen years and had seen all the ways students cheated. He patrolled the aisles of his classroom. He watched Frankie squirming in his seat. He knew even good students would often do desperate things when they weren't prepared. Frankie rolled his head around in a circle, sure he was trying to look at the answers of those around him. As Frankie moved his head a second time to loosen the muscles, Mr. Fugate came up behind him and snatched up Frankie's paper, ripping it in half.

"Hey, what'd you do that for?" Frankie shouted.

Mr. Fugate grinned. He loved catching students cheating. "I stood back there watching you cheat."

Frankie protested. "I never cheated." He stood up so quick his desk flipped over. Mr. Fugate grinned; he had him now. "Since you seem to want to throw things around, how about you head to the principal's office. I'll let him know you're on the way." Frankie looked around him. The other students kept their eyes on their paper. Frankie couldn't believe what he was hearing. He knew there was no sense arguing with the teacher. He grabbed his backpack and stomped out of the room. By the time he had walked to the office, Mr. Fugate had already filled the principal in on his version of what happened.

Frankie was not given much of a chance to say anything. Mr. Grimhold was waiting and was already on the phone with Frankie's dad. Frankie overheard the principal's side of the conversation as he sat in the office. "Yes, sir, your son was caught cheating in math.

When caught, he threw his desk across the room. This behavior will not be tolerated. You will need to pick your son up, he's suspended for ten days."

Frankie couldn't hold his tongue. He'd never been suspended or in trouble for anything throughout his school life. "Mr. Grimhold, that's not what happened, I never—"

Mr. Grimhold cut him off. "Just sit there and wait for your father." Frankie waited. Maybe his dad would be the voice of reason in this mess.

An hour later, Frankie's mom and dad walked into the office. Frankie jumped up. "Dad, I didn't do what they said I did. I wasn't cheating." Frankie looked at his dad and saw the color rise in his cheeks. He grabbed his son by the shirt and shoved him out the door.

"Give me the keys to your car, Frankie." They walked out of the office and to the parking lot. Frankie's mother got into the family car. His dad got into the driver seat of Frankie's car. "Dad, please, you have to listen to me."

"No, Frankie, I don't have to listen to you. We'll discuss this when we get home. You'll have plenty of time to think about what you did."

Frankie knew it was a bad sign that his dad was driving his car. He got into the front seat with his mom. One look at her tense face and Frankie knew there would be no conversation. When they pulled into their driveway, Frankie saw an unfamiliar car. He recognized the new preacher as he stepped out. Relief rushed over him. If Pastor Wingate had come to visit, his dad would have time to calm down before they talked. Maybe he would be able to make his dad understand what had happened. Frankie soon realized that would not be the case. His dad grabbed the pastor's hand and shook it. "I'm so glad you could come so quickly. We need your help with a situation." Frankie could not believe what he had just heard. His dad had called the pastor to talk to him? He knew it would not matter what he said.

Frankie sat on the couch, waiting while his dad and the preacher went into his office. He ran his fingers back-and-forth over the ridges in the fabric. Forced to sit there, it reminded him of the time he threw a ball through one of the windows, and his dad had made him sit there on that very couch to think about what he had done. He realized the punishment was not the actual spanking or yelling he would receive; it was the amount of time he had to sit and wait to see how he would be punished.

He was surprised to see his dad lead the pastor to the door instead of the living room where he'd been waiting. Frankie's father entered and sat in the chair across from him. "Frankie, I want you to listen to me before you decide to say anything and think carefully before you answer. Why weren't you prepared for the test and, then, think it okay to copy from someone else? That was the least of the things you did. I just can't believe my own son has turned so violent that he would throw a desk across the room at the teacher, out of anger. Why, Frankie? What would make you do something so violent? Are you doing drugs? We can work this out, if you are. We can get you help."

Frankie's mouth dropped open. He felt the bile from his stomach rise. It didn't matter what he said now. He had been tried and convicted even though he was innocent.

"I know it won't matter what I say to you now because you've already decided I'm guilty before hearing my side. I guess what I've always heard is true. I just chose not to believe it about my parents. Parents always tell their kids that they can tell them anything, and kids always say you can't. I've always sided with the parents. I thought that I had cool parents who would listen to me. I guess I was wrong." Frankie absentmindedly continued to run his fingers across the arm of the couch. "You listened to what the principal said, and then, just like the principal, you wouldn't let me say anything. Mr. Grimhold listened to the teacher and suspended me without letting me say a word. Even criminals get to tell their side of the story. Did you forget there are cameras in the classroom? Why didn't you ask to see the video? Is it so much easier to believe you have a violent son than to listen to his side of the story?" Frankie slammed his fist on the couch. His voice began to rise. "I've never given you any reason to doubt me. I've never broken the rules." Frankie looked at his dad sitting in the chair across from him with his left leg crossed over his right leg. His elbows rested on the chair arms, and his fingers came together to form a teepee. The scene could have been one of any psychiatrist sitting and listening to his patient.

Frankie grew angrier and instinctively struck out. "You know, Dad, I guess Grandpa was right. You are a coldhearted hothead. I understand now why he didn't let you have that car. You didn't believe him when someone told you he was having an affair. Someone at church told you they had seen him with another woman, and you jumped all over him. You believed that person over your own father. Then, you found out that Grandpa had picked up mom's sister to surprise her at lunch. Now you believe the people at the school over your own son. Funny, it always goes back to people at the church over your own family. If that's the case, I'm done with the church. You can have it." Frankie sat back, emotionally spent. He had expected his dad to say something to him throughout his tirade. Instead, his dad had sat there. He waited for his dad to say something. Frankie jumped to his feet. "Come on, Dad. Quit sitting there staring at me like I'm some delusional kid. Say something, yell at me, but don't just sit there."

Frankie's father slowly leaned forward. "Pastor Wingate told me just to pray about the situation until I'm calm enough to talk to you. I don't think I've reached that point yet. I'll give him a call and update him and see what he says about how I should handle this situation now. He is right about one thing. I've been too easy on my family. I need to start putting my foot down when it comes to you and your behavior. I've not disciplined you like people said I should. I always thought I had done the right thing and that you would turn out all right." He sat back, gripping the chair arms as if he needed to keep himself in place. Frankie could hear a tone in his voice he'd not heard in a long time—anger. "So Frankie, I'd like for you to go to your room and stay there until dinner. I don't want you on the phone with anyone. As a matter of fact, give me your cell phone. You're grounded from it until further notice. You're grounded from using your car until your suspension is over. Because you have chemistry labs that you will have to do, your mother will drive you to school each day at 3:00 p.m., and you will do the labs with the teacher. He's been generous enough to volunteer to help you so you don't get behind. I don't want to hear another word from you about this situation. We'll put it behind you and use it as a learning tool. Hopefully, you've learned that cheaters never get ahead. Go to your room and stay there."

Frankie got up and walked toward the hallway. He saw his mother standing in the doorway of her bedroom, listening. She ducked back in and shut the door. Had she been instructed not to talk to him? Frankie understood what Jacob had said about his dad being controlling. He hadn't believed Jacob when he said his dad would tell his friend's parents how to raise or handle their kids. Frankie now understood why kids didn't want to be Jacob's friend. But he wouldn't abandon Jacob. The kid needed someone to stand by him. After what had just happened to him, he could understand what it must be like to be a preacher's kid, always under the microscope.

Jacob dropped Tanya off and watched her run into the house. They'd heard that Frankie had been suspended. The news traveled quickly around the school. The rumors grew from Frankie getting caught cheating to punching out a teacher. In the short time Jacob had known Frankie, he knew he was extremely level-headed and would never do anything like he had been accused of. Tanya had talked with the kid who sat behind Frankie in his math class. The kid said the teacher had come up and snatched Frankie's paper and accused him of cheating. When he sent him to the office, he called the principal and accused him of throwing the desk. He said Frankie's desk tipped over when he stood up, but he'd never thrown it. Tanya had to talk to her parents and let them know the truth. First, she tried her mother, only to have the bedroom door slammed in her face. When she tried to speak to her dad, he refused. She couldn't understand what was going on with her family. They'd always been so happy and open. There had seldom been any trouble, at least, not for the last few years.

Dinner was quiet that night in the Bonita house. Frankie and Tanya had never seen their mother act the way she did, afraid to talk to her own children. She stared at her plate and only spoke when her husband commented. Frankie looked at his dad. "Can we talk about my suspension now?" His father continued to look at his wife, and she continued to stare at her plate. Something was going on, and Frankie and Tanya could feel it. Frankie tried again. "Dad, you never listened to my side of the story. All I was doing was stretching my neck, you know, doing a neck roll. I had a crick in my neck, but I never looked to the left or the right. I sure as heck didn't throw my desk. When Mr. Fugate told me to go to Principal Grimhold, I was angry. I stood up, and my desk tipped over. You know how those desks are. Besides, Dad, my desk is in the middle of a row. If I had been able to pick it up and throw it, I would have had to lift it over my head without hitting someone around me, and I would have had to throw it over three or four people. Now does that make sense to you?" His father continued to stare at his mother.

Frankie threw his fork on his plate and jumped up. "Sit down, Frankie." His father growled. "You will leave this table when everyone is done, and I tell you that you may leave. Do I make myself clear?" Frankie plopped down in the seat, folded his arms, and glared at his dad.

"Dad." Tanya tried. "Several kids in Frankie's class told me the teacher lied, including the kid sitting behind Frankie."

"Jose, maybe we need to do some further investigating. Maybe we need to ask to see the video from the cameras." Frankie's mom was cut short when her husband slammed his hand on the table.

"This is exactly what the pastor said would happen. He said whenever there is a problem with the kids, the mother always tries to baby them. He told me I wouldn't have a strong family until I learned to take control and all of you learned your place in this family." He glared at his wife. "You are to be in submission to me, Rosa. Are we clear on this?" His hand kept a steady rhythm with each emphasis.

"This is my house, and I am the head of it. All of you are here to follow my directions without question. This is the new rule in the house. If you follow the rules, we'll all get along." He slid his chair back and stormed from the room. His face was redder than they had ever seen it.

No one moved from the table. The food sat untouched, and tears slid down Tanya's face. Their mother slowly rose from her seat and began to clear the table. Frankie got up and grabbed the dishes from her hands. "I'll do the dishes, Mom. I'm sorry I caused so much trouble." His sister cleared the table while Frankie rinsed the dishes and placed them in the dishwasher. His mother continued to stand in the middle of the room. What had happened to turn her husband, their father, into the person they had just seen?

"I don't know where to go or what to do," she mumbled as she turned and walked out the back door of the Florida room. She had tried to get her husband to go easy on Frankie. She hadn't believed he had cheated. Her husband had agreed until he had called Pastor Wingate. After the phone call, her husband's attitude had changed.

Jose came out to check on his wife. He walked up behind her and wrapped his arms around her. She flinched and stiffened. She tried to relax, but it was useless. She stayed wrapped in his arms, unmoving. He slowly released his grip, and she stepped away.

"I'm sorry if I hurt your feelings. I'm just trying to be the best husband and father I can be. I know I sprung the change on you quickly. According to Pastor Wingate, we need to get things under control now." Jose waited for an answer from his wife. She nodded her head and continued to stand silent with her back toward him. Her husband turned, shoulders drooping, and returned to the house. He didn't understand how things could go so wrong. He was just doing what he was guided to do.

12

Ten days was a long time to be suspended. Tanya had visited each of Frankie's teachers with a request from his mother to email his lessons home. If he needed any handouts or books, Tanya was to pick them up. His days were filled with schoolwork and sitting in his room. His dad would check in on him to see what progress he had made. When Frankie had finished his lessons, he had to take his laptop to his dad. He'd even lost the privilege of using it. Anything that would give him pleasure was taken away. He had no game system, no television, or stereo. His dad had left a handful of books from the preacher and his Bible in his room. He had taken Frankie's phone so he could talk to no one.

Tanya worried about her brother. When Jacob came to pick her up for school, he knew something was wrong. She walked slowly toward the car; her lips pressed tightly together. She sat down with a sigh. Jacob tried to lighten things up. "That bad of a morning?" She smiled at him and fastened her seatbelt while biting her lower lip. "What's got you so worried?" Jacob asked.

Tanya looked at Jacob. Her eyes briefly flashed with anger. Was she angry with him? "I'm worried about Frankie. Dad has taken everything away except his Bible, a Bible study book, some religious books from your dad, and a Bible dictionary. He does his homework first thing in the morning and emails it to his teachers. Dad checks every few minutes so that he can make sure Frankie isn't doing anything besides homework. When he's done, Dad takes his computer and locks it in his office. Frankie won't talk to me or anyone. He hasn't shaved since he got suspended three days ago. All he does is sits in his room all day."

Jacob looked concerned. "That's not healthy."

"No, Jacob, it's not healthy," she snapped. He saw the anger flash in her eyes again. Was she blaming him for something? "My dad won't let him leave the room except to get the lunch my mom prepares ahead of time. He sits on the bed and stares at the wall. I've noticed he's started wearing long pajama pants."

Jacob looked confused. "What's wrong with wearing long pajama pants?"

Tanya hung her head and spoke softly. I'm afraid he may be hurting himself."

Jacob didn't want to come across as stupid, but he had to ask. "Hurt himself how?"

Tanya looked up, and Jacob could see tears running down her cheeks. "I went to empty his garbage and found tissue with blood on it."

"I wouldn't worry about it. It could have been from a nosebleed."

"You don't understand. Before my dad became a Christian, he used to drink a lot. He'd take his anger out on Frankie. He never hit him, but he would yell at him a lot. He was verbally abusive to all of us. Frankie tried to act like nothing was wrong. One day, I walked in on him after Dad had one of his outbursts, and I found Frankie with a pin poking his thigh. He was angry, and he took it out on himself. I'm afraid he may be doing that again."

Jacob got a glimpse of what Tanya wasn't saying to him. "So your dad used to have a temper, stopped after he became a Christian, and now his temper is back. Is that what you've been trying to tell me?" Tanya nodded. "Let me guess, the temper returned after my dad came and talked with your dad about Frankie." Tanya didn't answer right away. "He did come over and advise him, didn't he?" Tanya looked out the side window and nodded. "Why didn't you tell me?"

Tanya flipped her head around. "Because I was afraid you would get upset with me and tell me it wasn't his fault."

Jacob pulled into his parking spot and shut off the car. He turned and took Tanya's hand. "Let me tell you something. Remember I told you it was difficult being a PK? Well, now you understand why. No one wants to be my friend because my dad has to put his two cents worth into everything. He always criticized my friends, telling them what he thought of what they said or did. How long would you want to be my friend knowing everything you did was going to be watched and critiqued by my father? The kids at church stopped hanging around with me because my dad would tell their parents how to handle any disruptive behavior. If they avoided me, then, my dad wasn't in their lives."

Tanya leaned over and kissed Jacob lightly on the lips. "I'll still be here. I won't let what your father does turn me against you. I know my brother won't either. We've got to find a way to cheer him up. Why don't you see if your dad will let you come and visit Frankie? He can call my dad and tell him that maybe you would be a good influence on Frankie."

"We can give it a try," Jacob said. He didn't believe that he could have much influence on his dad's decisions. There was a better chance his dad would not want him around Frankie because he might be considered a bad influence. The day passed quickly, and Jacob dropped Tanya off. He decided to approach his dad before he grew cold feet. Jacob knocked on the office door and waited until his dad invited him in.

"Jacob, what can I do for you?" His dad looked up from his notepad.

"Dad, I know Frankie is struggling in math. If not, he wouldn't have gotten into trouble. Do you think you could call his dad and talk to him for me? I'm willing to tutor him in math to help him out." He stood, fidgeting, placing his hands first in his pockets, then pulling them out.

"Jacob, I'm proud of you, that's an excellent idea. I know it's difficult being the son of a preacher and to have lasting friends. I think Frankie and Tanya are wonderful young people. Most importantly, I believe you can be a great influence on them." Jacob stood dumbfounded. It had worked. He stood there as his dad called and made the arrangements. "They're expecting you in about thirty minutes. Thanks a lot, Jacob. You've made me very proud. You're finally maturing." Jacob nodded his head and left the office. He grabbed his math book and a snack before heading out to his car.

Mr. Bonita let Jacob into the house and sent him to Frankie's room. "Hey, Frankie," Jacob said with a smile as he opened the door. Frankie was shocked to see someone standing in his doorway.

"Hey, Jacob. How'd you get past the gestapo?" Jacob just shrugged and entered the room, closing the door.

"Your sister decided I needed to tutor you in math." Jacob grinned. "Get your math book out, and let's get started."

Frankie glared at Jacob. He didn't need a tutor. "Listen, Jacob, I don't care what my dad said, I don't need a math tutor." He stayed on his bed in defiance."

"Frankie, get your math book and come over here." Jacob tried to sound stern, but instead, his voice had a giggly hiccup to it.

"What are you up to, Jacob?" Frankie asked.

"Well, if you ever get over here, then maybe we can get started, and you'll see."

Frankie brought his math book to the desk. Jacob pulled some math papers from his book. "Copy these quickly and hand them back. Only copy the ones I circled." Frankie finished the job and waited. Jacob had just returned the papers to the inside of his book when they heard footsteps. Jacob snatched Frankie's paper from him and pretended to study it. As the door began to open, Jacob started to talk. "These look good. I think you finally understand this concept."

Mr. Bonita popped his head into the room. "How's it going, boys?"

Jacob quickly answered, "Great. I think Frankie finally understands linear equations."

Frankie chimed in, "I get them now. All the problems he just gave me are right. I didn't understand the formula, that was the problem. I think I'll do better with Jacob helping me. Thanks."

Mr. Bonita pushed the bedroom door open further and looked around. You two have been at it for quite some time. I think it's time you took a break and hung outside together." He turned and walked back down to his office. As soon as they heard his door shut, Frankie slugged Jacob in the shoulder. "Hey, man, that was fast thinking."

Jacob slugged him back. "Hey, you need to thank your sister. She's the one who told me what you were going through. Besides, I feel kind of guilty because my dad was the one who talked to your dad. I knew you'd be in more trouble." Jacob looked down at his shoes. "I wouldn't be surprised if you decided you wanted nothing more to do with me."

"I don't know what your dad said to my dad, Jacob, but my dad's trashing all of us."

Jacob stood up. "Let's go outside to continue this conversation." They walked into the kitchen and grabbed Tanya on the way out to the dock. Frankie and Tanya sat down. Jacob stood in front of them with his hands on his hips. He tried to put a stern look on his face. "Let me tell you something. This is my family, and I am the head of it. God expects you to listen to me. You need to know your place and stay in it." He looked at Tanya and Frankie. "So how close was I?"

Tanya spoke first. "Oh my gosh, those were almost the exact words that came out of my dad's mouth last night. How did you know?"

Jacob sat down and laughed. "That's the speech he gives everyone. He doesn't feel he has control of his own family, so he has to try to make everyone else do this. That way, he can feel like a success." Jacob leaned back, soaking in the sun.

Frankie leaned forward. "That's just wrong. I'm so glad I am not you and that he is not my dad. I hope he got whatever he thought he wanted out of his system." Jacob refused to look up or answer. He knew his dad, and there was no way his dad would give up. He had to be in control of everything because the one thing he wanted to control—his own family—he couldn't.

The three teens walked back to the house. Frankie's dad was waiting for them. "I think you need to head on home. It's time for Frankie to help his mom, and then, it's back to his room to study." Jacob left the house and headed home. The rest of Frankie's suspension went faster. Every night, Jacob came to help him with his math. It gave him the little break he needed to make it each day.

13

Frankie dreaded the return to school more than anything. He had never been suspended before. He knew he'd have to go through the same ribbing he had given others when they returned. His day was not as bad as he figured it would be, until he entered Mr. Fugate's class.

"Well, Mr. Bonita, I see you've decided to grace us with your presence. I do hope you've learned it's not right to cheat." Frankie could feel himself getting angry, but he chose not to answer or look at Mr. Fugate. He took out his materials for the class.

"Oh no, you don't, Mr. Bonita. You get a front-row seat so that I can make sure you never cheat again." He could see a sneer forming on Mr. Fugate's face. Frankie carefully extricated himself from the desk. He couldn't afford to knock it over again and be accused of throwing the desk again. He sauntered to the front desk. Even this seemed to irritate his teacher. Frankie knew, no matter what he did, he would be on Mr. Fugate's radar. What he didn't understand was why.

When Frankie got home, his dad was waiting for him. "So how was your first day back?" Frankie heard the irritation in his dad's voice.

He replied, "It was just fine." He tried to walk past his father but was stopped when his dad stepped in front of him and motioned Frankie to sit on the couch.

"How about you tell me the truth this time." Frankie had no idea what his dad was referring to.

"Really, Dad, it was a great day." He began to worry. Why was his dad acting like this?

"Frankie, I know exactly how your day went. Mr. Fugate called and said you have a bad attitude, refused to work, and argued with him." Frankie started to protest and was cut off. "You will either change this attitude, or we'll have to find a way to change it."

Frankie tried hard to keep his mouth shut. What did Mr. Fugate have against him?

"I swear to you that I didn't have a problem in his class. I don't know what he's talking about. I went to class. He told me to move to the front row, and I did. I sat and did all of my work and didn't say a word."

"Exactly," his father said. "He said you didn't participate in the conversations at all." Frankie knew that he was going to have a very long year in math, unless he could figure out what Mr. Fugate's problem was. His dad dismissed him to his room. He did his homework while waiting for dinner to be served. Once again, dinner was eaten in silence. No one wanted to suffer another tirade from their dad.

With the meal finished, Frankie stood to remove his dishes. He farther spoke up. "Just where do you think you're going? This is what I'm talking about, Frankie. You show no courtesy for anyone. You're just rude. Did I tell you that you could get up from the table?" Tanya and her mother sat frozen in their chair. What had brought this on? Frankie sat back down. "Say something, Frankie. Tell me why you refuse to do what God commands you to do?"

Frankie had finally had enough. He was through being accused of things he hadn't done. He slammed his hands on the table and pushed himself up. "I don't know what it is you think God has commanded me to do. It seems that the only one around here who knows what God wants us to do anymore is you. I guess the rest of us will end up in hell because we can't figure it out on our own. After all, we just aren't as holy as you are."

Frankie's father reached out and grabbed his son and shoved him down into the chair. "You will never speak to me that way. The sooner you learn who is in charge here, the better things will go for you."

Frankie lashed out. "Just what do you think you're in charge of, Dad, or didn't the preacher tell you that yet? Maybe he hasn't told you because he has to wait for God to tell him before he can tell you."

"Frankie," hissed his mother. She didn't know what was happening with her family anymore. They had not argued like this for several years. Frankie turned to look at his mother when he suddenly found himself falling backward.

Tanya began to cry. Her dad had never raised a hand to any of them, even when he had been drinking. This behavior from her father terrified her, and she ran from the table to her room. Her father yelled at her to return. Instead, she locked her door.

He began to give orders. "Rosa, get these dishes done up, now. Don't even try to defend the kids. You know as well as I do they are becoming defiant and out of hand. I'll put them back in their place. Rosa stood and cleared the dishes. Frankie get your butt in your room and don't move until time for school tomorrow." Frankie picked himself up from the floor and went to his room, shutting and locking his door. He didn't want anyone coming in. He pulled the pushpin off the bulletin board and began.

The first prick was painful. Each prick after that brought relief. He thought about the change in his dad. Had his dad started drinking again? This was his behavior before he gave up alcohol. Something wasn't right. The more he thought about his dad, the angrier he got. He found himself scratching letters in his leg. He would scratch his feelings out, and that way, he would always remember how he felt. First, he scratched out the word *hate*. At that moment, he hated what his dad was doing. Then, he scratched the word *anger*. He sat, poking more holes in his leg after he had finished scratching in the letters. He wiped the drops of blood from his leg with a tissue. He removed the peroxide from the bathroom cabinet and used a little bit of it to clean the wounds he had created. He looked at his clock. It was only eight o'clock in the evening, but he was exhausted. Maybe he could talk with Mr. Fugate the next morning.

Frankie arrived early and met Jacob and Tanya. He explained to them what he planned to do. Tanya was skeptical. It would be his word against Mr. Fugate again.

"I've got an idea," Jacob said. He ran back to his car and took out a small handheld recorder. Tape your class, and then, if the same thing happens tonight, you have the proof you need.

"You've got some pretty cool ideas in that noggin of yours," Frankie said, knocking on Jacob's head.

Frankie was the first one in his class. He sharpened his pencils, putting one on his desk and one in his pocket with the tape recorder. He opened his book, took out his homework, and sat waiting. The bell rang, and students began to fill up the seats. Mr. Fugate collected homework and, then, proceeded with the lesson. Frankie took down notes as fast as he could. His pencil's lead broke, and Frankie reached into his pocket at the same time, Mr. Fugate turned and looked at him.

"Mr. Bonita, would you mind showing me what you are playing with in your pocket?" Frankie pressed the play button before he pulled out the pencil.

"My lead broke, Mr. Fugate, and I was just getting out my second pencil." He kept his tone as even as possible.

"Liar. I've been watching you. You've done nothing all period except goof off."

Frankie couldn't believe Mr. Fugate would say something like that. It was an outright lie. "What have you got to say now?" Mr. Fugate asked.

Frankie willed himself to stay calm. "I'm sorry, if that's what you thought, Mr. Fugate. I've been taking down the notes and working the problems with you. I needed another pencil because my lead broke. If that was distracting, I apologize." Frankie could hear a twitter of laughter circulating around the room. Mr. Fugate slammed the book in his hand down on Frankie's desk. "To the office," he yelled. Frankie was getting used to this procedure. He picked up all of his work and slid it into the proper folder. He placed the pencil back in his pocket and walked toward the door.

Mr. Fugate wasn't quite finished with Frankie. "Is that how all you grease balls operate? You have a story for everything, it seems." Frankie continued to walk out the door toward the office. When he reached the principal's office, Mr. Grimhold was already on the phone with Mr. Fugate.

When he had finished speaking with the teacher, the principal turned and talked to Frankie. "What is it about Mr. Fugate's class that makes you misbehave?" Frankie opened his mouth to answer and was quickly told to close it. He was sent to in-school suspension for the rest of the day. As he left the office, he could hear the principal dialing his phone. He knew the call was going to his father. As Frankie stepped into the hallway, he reached into his pocket and turned off the recorder. Maybe this would exonerate him.

When Frankie arrived home, his father was waiting for him. He wouldn't let him play the recording. He was sent to his room for the rest of the evening with no dinner. Frankie no longer cared. He replayed the tape. He had evidence his teacher didn't like him because of his race. Frankie didn't know his mom was in the hallway and had heard the tape while he played it. She decided to confront the principal. It might mean she got in trouble with her husband, but she needed to show Frankie some support. Just the day before, she had read about a teen who had finally had enough bullying at school. He came home from school one day and blew his brains out. She didn't want that to happen to her son. She'd just have to take her chances with her husband.

CHAPTER

14

Mrs. Bonita drove to the school early the next morning. She asked to speak with Mr. Grimhold and was shown to his office. She introduced herself and came to the point. "Mr. Grimhold, I'm Frankie Bonita's mother. I'm here because I am very concerned about my son." Before she could say anything else, she was cut off.

"We are all concerned about your son, Mrs. Bonita. His constant outbursts in his math class are getting out of hand. If he continues, we may have to expel him." Mrs. Bonita sat quiet, lips pressed tightly shut. Mr. Grimhold had seen that look before. He wasn't new to dealing with mothers who babied their children in high school. He had never met Frankie's mother and was not prepared for this demure-looking woman.

"Mr. Grimhold, you seem to have some things backward here, so let me help you clear them up. I want a copy of the video the day my son was suspended. I want a conference with all of his teachers this afternoon. I am not going to argue this point with you. If I don't have an agreement with you before I walk out of this school, then, I will make three stops on my way home. The first will be to the school board. If I have to file a grievance against you, the school, and Mr. Fugate. I will. The second stop will be to my attorney, where I will file harassment and bullying charges against this school and the school board. Finally, I will stop by the local paper and find a reporter who is willing to listen to my case. With all of the anti-bullying campaigns going on, do you think I won't find a sympathetic ear with the press?" She sat back and folded her hands in her lap and waited. The ball was now in his court.

"Mrs. Bonita, I understand how upset you are. I assure you I am doing everything in my power to help your son. I communicate daily with your husband. I let him know what is going on each day in each of his classes. It seems to me that the breakdown is in the communication between you and your husband. I assure you I've done everything in my power to accommodate your family, according to the school board guidelines. Please feel free to do whatever you feel you need to do. I'm sure our attorneys can handle it. Now if you'll excuse me, I have hall duty." He stood up and walked out of his office, leaving her sitting by herself.

As Mrs. Bonita walked out of the office, she ran into her daughter. "Mom, what are you doing here?"

"Tanya, were you aware that Frankie had a tape of his math teacher calling him a derogatory name?"

"I knew Frankie took Jacob's tape recorder to class. He was going to talk with Mr. Fugate to see if he could figure out what the problem was. I didn't know he had taped anything. Frankie avoids me anymore." She looked at her mother's worried face.

"Tanya, I have one more question for you. Were you aware that all of his teachers are reporting to the principal each day and that he is reporting to your dad each day?" The horrified look on Tanya's face said it all.

Tanya wondered why they would do that to her brother? He had always been a good student.

"Mom, I don't know what is going on anymore. I'll talk to some of the kids in his classes and see if I can get some information from them." Mrs. Bonita hugged her daughter and walked out of the school.

When she arrived home, her husband was waiting for her. He held the door open for her and followed her inside. "You just couldn't trust me to do what is best for our son, could you? Is this what our marriage has come to? I told you I would handle this. I'm the head of this house, not you. Leave it alone and let me do my job. You do yours. Be the housewife God told you to be."

Mrs. Bonita had finally had enough. "I am the wife God told me to be. I am the wife that stood beside her drunken, abusive husband for years when so many others were leaving theirs. I will not stand here and watch you turn back into that abusive husband again." She turned and walked off. Mr. Bonita had seen the flash of anger in her eyes and knew better than to cross her when she was like that. He left the house and went to work, leaving her without a resolution to their problems.

15

Jacob tried to avoid talking to his dad while Frankie was suspended. His dad questioned him every evening. He tried to make things sound as positive as possible. Once Frankie returned to school, things at home became tense. His father would talk about the "situation" at the Bonita home. Jacob knew better than to say anything in reply to his dad. He didn't want to start an argument.

After dinner, Jacob helped his mom with the garden. They had created the stepping stones. His mom had painted words on each one, and he had sealed them for her. They had begun to place them along the path Jacob had dug from the back door to the swing. He helped his mom plant a variety of flowering plants and ornamental grasses along the border edges of the path. He walked toward his mom with one of the last stones.

"Is Frankie okay, Jacob? His mom called me today and was upset. She said things are falling apart over there. She couldn't say anything more because her husband walked in. I quickly asked her to lunch tomorrow because I heard her husband ask her who she was talking to on the phone. She told me she'd have to get back to me after she checked her calendar. Then, she hung up."

Frankie stopped what he was doing and stretched as he looked toward the house. When he was sure his dad was nowhere around, he began to tell her what was going on. "It's bad, Mom. Did you know dad went over and talked to Mr. Bonita? He is advising him on ways to handle his family. Mr. Bonita is telling his family that he is in charge, and they are all to listen and follow his rules. Does that sound familiar?"

His mom stood up and walked to the swing. Jacob followed and sat beside her. She grabbed her sketchbook off the side table in case her husband came out. "I was afraid of that. When he told me we were moving, he started acting like he was the only one in charge. I had no say in anything. I don't really know what is bothering him, but something is. He gets this way when he has something big on his mind. I just wish I knew what it was."

Jacob listened to his mom. She rarely shared things like this with him. "I feel terrible for Mrs. Bonita, Mom. She heard a tape Frankie made of Mr. Fugate going off on him in class. She tried to tell Frankie's dad, and he ignored her. She tried to talk to the principal, and he ignored her and called her husband. Tanya told me her dad is acting the way he did when he was drinking. She said she's actually afraid of him. I don't know what to do to help her or Frankie."

His mom leaned over and put her arm around him. "I know exactly what you mean. I don't know how to help or advise their mom and, at the same time, keep our husbands from yelling at us. I guess all we can do is pray."

They sat in the swing until the sun began to go down, then went into the house.

CHAPTER

16

Frankie knew it was wrong to skip class. He just couldn't take school anymore. Since it was the last class of the day, it was easier just to leave the school campus. He'd go back to the cabin. He'd been driving around one day when he had found the fishing shack. It was the perfect place to hide. He was away from his father and all the others who were giving him grief. After doing a little research, he had learned the fishing shack had been an old slave cabin. It was the perfect place to hang out.

He turned his car onto a small dirt path. Unless you knew the road was there, you would drive right past it. No markers identified this forgotten relic of the Civil War era. About a quarter of a mile down the path, Frankie stopped his car. He could drive no farther. Everything was so overgrown that you had to walk the last few hundred feet down a well-worn path to the cabin. This was good because your car couldn't be seen from the road or the river. Younger kids avoided the quaint cabin out of fear. They called it the haunted fishing shack. Teens had passed down stories for years about ghosts they had seen at the shack. There were urban legends. Some were told about slaves that were killed and fed to the alligators. Other stories were told of drunken fishermen who got too close to the water at night and became food for the alligators. Frankie didn't believe in ghosts, so the stories didn't bother him.

The shack had been built on top of large boulders that sat slightly offshore. This served two purposes. It kept the water from rising into the shack when the river flooded. It also allowed easy access to the river by canoe or small boat. Both ends of the cabin had two windows. Each window had one large shutter held in place by a turn peg at the top. When released, the shutters folded down against the side of the cabin. The cabin had two doors. The first was on the east end between two of the windows and provided access from the woods or the small porch where a small boat could be docked. Frankie had added a padlock to it a long time ago. This kept everyone out that he didn't want in.

The second door was on the river side. It was a crude version of narrow French doors. They could be opened to allow the air to pass through. This shack had it all. It allowed terrific airflow and panoramic views of the river or the Spanish moss-draped cypress trees. It also contained a piece of history that most people preferred was forgotten. Inside, the cabin was modestly furnished. It included a small cook stove, a cot, and a small table with chairs to accommodate four people. This cabin was unlike any other. Along one of the walls were iron shackles. Someone had put in a lot of effort to turn this old slave shack into a fishing cabin. For some reason, they had left the slave manacles attached to the wall. Frankie had done some research and found the cabin had been one of twenty slave cabins along the river. It was the only one left standing. Slaves were chained to the walls at night so they couldn't slip into the water and escape. Frankie found this bit of history to be both fascinating and gruesome.

He carried his backpack into the cabin and started to unpack. He took out a six-pack of beer and stashed it in the cooler he kept in the corner. It had been easy for him to score the beer. He knew the man at the little mom-and-pop store sold alcohol to minors. He also knew the guy had already been in trouble with the cops. The sheriff was a member of Frankie's church, and all it took was one threat to turn him in, and he was able to buy the beer. Frankie didn't really like the taste of beer. He drank it because he knew it was in defiance of his dad. Anything he could do that would be against his dad's wishes was what he wanted to do. He popped the tab on the first beer and drank it down.

Frankie returned home at nine o'clock that evening. He knocked on his sister's window, and she let him in. She could smell the alcohol on his breath. "Frankie, Dad is furious. You skipped school today. He's talking about taking your car away from you." He didn't answer her. Instead, he went straight to his room, took a shower, and went to bed.

CHAPTER 17

The next morning, Frankie was one of the first ones up. He ate a quick breakfast and went to school. He stopped one of his friends from math and got the homework assignment, then sat down and quickly pumped out the work. He was sitting at one of the tables alone, reviewing his history notes, when his father showed up.

"Are you trying to flunk math class, Frankie?" Frankie looked at his dad like he didn't know what he was talking about. "I got a call again yesterday that you weren't in math class. How are you going to pass if you don't do the work?"

Frankie reached into his backpack and pulled out his homework. "You mean this work? The work he assigned yesterday after going over linear equations for the umpteenth time? I got it, Dad. I'm not sure that you understand this teacher is out to get me. I'm not even sure you care. But that's okay because I've got my own back. I learned when I was little that I had to watch my own back because you never did." He stood and quickly headed inside. The last thing he wanted was a shouting match with his dad in public.

He stepped into the hall and was confronted by both Mr. Fugate and Mr. Grimhold. They marched him down to Mr. Fugate's room. Mr. Fugate started in on Frankie. "I want you to know that I will not accept your late homework from yesterday. You want to skip my class, you get no credit."

Frankie looked from him to the principal and waited for the principal to speak. "Mr. Fugate is trying to be very fair with you. You just don't seem to want to pass his class. Your constant outbursts, your defiance, and now you're not doing your work. You're determined to fail his class. What do you have to say about all of this?" his principal asked.

He looked at Mr. Fugate, a slight grin on his face. "So you're telling me the work I turned in yesterday won't be counted? What about the homework I did last night?" He reached into his backpack and pulled out his homework, along with his notebook with all of the class notes. "I decided to sit in the back yesterday. I'm tired of being your target. I passed my paper up along with everyone else. If you don't believe it, pull out the classwork and check. He waited while Mr. Fugate pulled the work from his homework bin. In the middle of the stack was Frankie's homework. "I copied these notes and problems from your board, Mr. Fugate." He showed the notebook to the principal and Mr. Fugate. "I also completed all of my homework," he said as he showed it to them. "I am not going to sit in front of the class and have you harass me anymore. I've already told my mom how you try to humiliate me every day. You call me dumb, grease ball, and greaser. I am not the only Hispanic in the classroom. We don't know where this is coming from or why you're targeting us." Frankie turned to Mr. Grimhold. "Trust me on something. The other day, when my mother came in to complain, and you blew her off, you made a mistake. She's like a mama bear protecting her cubs. She'll do whatever it takes to solve this bullying. That's something I can promise you." He sat back with his hands behind his head, surveying the two men.

Mr. Fugate's face was beet red. "This, Mr. Grimhold, is the defiance I am talking about. He's constantly making accusations."

Frankie interrupted him, "No, Mr. Fugate, I'm not making accusations. In this day and age, you seem to forget electronic devices capture all kinds of things. My mom has plenty of evidence." He watched Mr. Fugate turn from red to purple.

"Mr. Grimhold, are you going to allow him to sit there and make threats?"

Mr. Grimhold wasn't sure where he should go with this. Was it possible that the boy's mom really did have evidence? If she did and he dismissed her the way he had, then, his job could be in jeopardy. He had to think and act quickly. "Frankie, hand me your cell phone."

Frankie looked at him. "I don't have a cell phone with me. My dad makes me leave it in the car. He said there's never a reason I need to bring it into the school. It would only be a distraction. If you'd like, I can walk to the car and get it for you."

Mr. Fugate was fuming. "I'm sure he's lying. Check his backpack." Frankie dumped his backpack, spilling two textbooks, a binder, and several pens and pencils onto the desk. Mr. Fugate insisted they walk him to the car to find the phone. Frankie agreed. As he got to his car, Tanya and Jacob were pulling in. He waved to them and smiled. They stayed in the car, watching from a distance as Frankie pulled out his phone and handed it to the principal. A couple of minutes later, he placed it back into his car, and they all walked off.

Frankie made sure he was in math class that day, sitting in the back. He didn't talk to anyone because he didn't want them to be the next target. When his paper was returned, there was a big fat zero on it. In bright-red letters was the word *plagiarized*. He raised his hand and asked how he had gotten a zero and who he had copied it from. Mr. Fugate was sure Frankie had no phone on him since he was a witness to it being left in his car. There were no other recording devices either. After all, he had been through Frankie's backpack, and there was nothing in it.

"Well, since you seem to be dumber than dirt, I knew you had to have copied from someone. I don't know who, but we all know Mexican's are nothing but a bunch of tomato pickers." There was an audible gasp in the classroom.

"Well, Mr. Fugate, obviously I'm not the dumb one. I know the difference between a Mexican and a Puerto Rican, which is what I am." Giggling flittered around the room. Mr. Fugate shot an angry look around the classroom. He had obviously lost control, and it was evident with his next comment.

Mr. Fugate's response was angry. "It really doesn't matter, Mr. Bonita. We all know that your people think with their pants and not their head. That's why you're all a lying bunch of slobs. You can't find things on your own, not even your own women. You've got to steal from honest, hard-working white people. I don't want to see you in my class anymore. Leave. I don't care where you go as long as it isn't here. You make me want to puke." Frankie stood and announced he would be going to the principal's office. His backpack slid off his shoulder, dropping next to Kevin's desk. Kevin handed it back to him, slipping the tape recorder into it.

Frankie headed down the hallway toward the office. It was a coincidence he saw his sister coming back from the library. Frankie stopped her and handed her the tape recorder to hold for him. He didn't want any evidence when he went to the principal's office.

As Frankie walked into the office, the lady at the front desk shook her head. She'd never known this boy to be a troublemaker in all the years she had known him. It seemed funny that none of the other teachers had an issue with him. Mr. Fugate had only been with them for two years. It seemed strange that the only kids Mr. Fugate ever sent to the office were Hispanic kids. She kept her nose out of it, never saying anything about her observation. She needed her job and didn't want to cause herself any trouble.

Frankie waited outside Mr. Grimhold's office. He stepped out, took one look at Frankie, and went back in. Frankie sat there until his dad showed up. "Frankie, I'm getting tired of coming down here every day. What did you do this time?" Frankie didn't bother answering because he knew whatever he said would be completely different than what his dad would be told. Mr. Grimhold called his dad into the office. When he came out, his face was beet-red. "They're talking about expelling you this time." Frankie sat there and said nothing. "Meet me at home," he said, then whirled out of the office.

Frankie walked to the front desk. "Thank you for being so kind and nonjudgmental, Mrs. Brownley."

She had to ask him before he was gone. "Frankie, why didn't you try to defend yourself?"

"I've been trying to do that for the last month, and it doesn't matter what I say, no one believes me. Why should I waste my breath? It only makes them angrier." He smiled at her and walked out.

When Frankie returned home, his dad was waiting in the drive. "Give me the keys, Frankie." He handed them to his father without a word. He knew what was going on, so why fight it? Frankie didn't come to the dinner table that night. He stayed in his room. His mother tried to bring him some dinner, but her husband stopped her. She could see the gap in their family getting wider.

18

Sunday morning should have been a relief from the stress Jacob and his mom had been feeling at home. Nothing could have been further from the truth. Jacob sat with Frankie and Tanya at the back of the church. He never knew what his dad was going to preach on. His dad didn't believe in sharing it with him or his mom before Sunday.

Jacob cringed when his father started his sermon. "We have become a rebellious nation. This is nothing new. It can be traced back to the first family. Adam and Eve rebelled against God by eating the forbidden fruit. Cain rebelled by killing his brother. In the '60s, we began questioning authority. Our kids talk back. There is no respect. Families are further undermined by non-submissive wives. God gave couples two directives. The wives were to submit to their husband's authority, and husbands were to love their wives. If a man lets his wife rule the house and undermine his authority and he does not correct her, then, he shows he does not love her."

Jacob had heard enough. He put on his game face and began to think up lyrics to a song in his head. He had done this for years. His dad was becoming more and more confrontational. He knew his dad didn't care what the people thought. Only he knew what God wanted him to tell them. They didn't have to like him; they needed only follow what he said God wanted.

Jacob stood at the car after church and watched the congregation file out. Whenever his dad gave this sermon—which was often—the scene was the same. The women marched out with scowls on their faces, and the men had smiles. Jacob folded his arms and leaned back against the car. He watched as Frankie's family left the church, tension written on their faces. Jacob's father came out and locked up the church. As he climbed into the car, his mom refused to comment on the sermon. Jacob could see her jaw working as she clenched her teeth to keep from saying anything. She would give his dad the silent treatment.

Jacob ate his lunch, watching his mom with amusement. Whenever his dad requested something, she got it, handed it to her husband, and curtsied with her head bowed before she sat down. As much as Jacob loved watching his mom's performance, he knew it was only a matter of time before his dad would get mad and start yelling. He could have counted down the seconds. When he began shouting, his mom stood up and removed their plates from the table. Jacob looked at his father's stunned face. His dad had finished neither his lunch or his coffee. When he protested, her reply was simple. "I'm being submissive and doing my wifely duties." Jacob wanted to laugh, but he didn't want to suffer his dad's wrath now that he was mad at his mom. He asked to be excused and went to his room. Jacob called Tanya, and their family invited him over. He told his parents where he was going and left.

When Jacob arrived, Frankie and Tanya met him in the drive. They slid into his car. He looked surprised. He had assumed they were going to visit there. Frankie gave Jacob directions to the cabin. Tanya had only been to the cabin a couple of times. Frankie had made sure he had replaced the beer with sodas before he had invited them out.

Jacob was surprised by how remote the cabin was. He loved the isolation. If he could ever get his own place, he would love something secluded like this. He could write his music and be at one with nature. Frankie pulled out the sodas and gave one to each of them. They sat and talked about school and how to get even with Mr. Fugate before heading back home.

As Jacob pulled into Frankie's drive, he noticed his dad's car. He walked inside with Frankie and Tanya. Frankie's father stood up.

"Great, just the three we needed to talk with." Frankie was concerned. His dad had gone from this sullen man to someone who acted as if they had no cares at all.

"Frankie, we're going to have a house guest for a couple of weeks next month. Jacob will be staying with us while his parents take a group of people to the Holy Land." Once again, Jacob was the last to know of a change in his life. Why did his dad have such a hard time telling him things? The three teens stood there and said nothing.

Jacob knew what the adults were thinking. Frankie's dad thought Jacob would be an incredible influence on Frankie. Jacob's dad felt he didn't have to worry about Jacob for a while because Mr. Bonita was a hard-working deacon in the church.

Pastor Wingate and his wife said their goodbyes and walked out with Jacob. When they were finally home, Jacob stormed into the house. As his dad walked in, Jacob turned on him. "Thanks a lot, Dad. You still, don't trust me enough to tell me things without an audience?"

His dad answered in a monotone voice. "It has nothing to do with that. I just knew that you had no say in this matter. Your mother and I will be going to the Holy Land, and you needed a place to stay. There was no reason to discuss anything with you."

Jacob felt his face turning red. "You know, Dad, I am almost seventeen. You don't trust me enough to stay home for a week or two by myself?"

"Actually, Jacob, I don't," he said. "With your recent outbursts, you haven't shown me that you're mature enough to stay at home or make any decisions on your own. I didn't need to consult you. You're still a child, and I am the adult."

Jacob turned and went to his room. It wasn't that he didn't want to stay at Frankie's house. It was the principle of it. His dad had made a decision and not said anything to him. He hadn't even known his dad was planning a trip to the Holy Land. Once again, he felt isolated and alone. Had his mom known about this in advance, or was she blindsided like he was? It didn't really matter anymore.

CHAPTER

19

The weeks flew by. Frankie was excited to know Jacob would be staying with them for two weeks. He figured his dad wouldn't want something terrible to get back to the preacher, so things should lighten up around the house. Tanya was excited to know her boyfriend would be staying with them. She would get to see him every day and every night. She would have to keep her emotions in check, or her dad might change his mind.

Jacob showed up at school with everything he needed to take to Frankie's house stored in the trunk of his car. Jacob's dad had given him twenty dollars for whatever he might want to spend it on. His dad had given money for food and other essentials to Frankie's dad. Good thing Jacob had his own bank account, or he wouldn't be able to buy gas for his car.

The school day went quickly, and Jacob soon found himself at Frankie's house. He tried to help out, but they wouldn't let him do anything. He, Frankie, and Tanya sat at the kitchen table and did their homework in record time. They went out to the dock until dinner was ready, and their talk drifted to school.

"Man, I don't know what to do about Mr. Fugate. I think he wants me out of his class at all cost. But I'm determined to stick it out. I've stopped trying to convince my dad that Mr. Fugate is out to get me, but I know Mom's on my side. My mom has every recording that was recorded during class of him calling me names."

Jacob shook his head in disbelief. "They haven't done anything about it?"

Tanya put her hand on Frankie's knee. "Mom tried to talk to the school. She even filed a grievance with the school board, but nothing happened," Frankie said. "Several of my friends in the class tried talking with the principal. Instead of listening to them, he accused me of provoking them to say slanderous things about Mr. Fugate. They wrote up statements and gave them to my mom. They were the ones recording Mr. Fugate and passing it on to Tanya. They search my backpack daily. I continue to sit in the back, do my work, and turn it in, and I am still failing his class. It really makes me angry that my dad never questions any of it."

Jacob was getting used to the situation at Frankie's house. He could see Mr. Bonita treat Frankie one way, and when Jacob was out of the way, he treated Frankie different. Wednesday was no different than being at home with his parents. Jacob knew that he would still be required to go to church on Wednesday. After all, how would it look if the deacon didn't take the preacher's kid to church? As soon as the service was over, Frankie and Jacob left while Tanya stayed behind with her mother. They were practicing with the church choir. Frankie decided to go to the old fishing shack. He hadn't been there after dark for quite some time. They sat on the porch for a while, watching the alligators swim by. Jacob felt nervous sitting on the porch. He knew it sat only twelve inches above the water. An alligator could easily climb out. He sipped his soda in silence. He had turned down a beer Frankie had offered him. Frankie teased him. The truth was Jacob hated the taste of alcohol.

A thick fog began to roll in, so Jacob suggested they head back home. The fog was so thick in some areas, it was difficult to see. Frankie came around a curve and was suddenly blinded by oncoming lights enhanced by the mist. As the car passed him, he suddenly saw a bicycle in front of him. Frankie swerved but was not quick enough. He heard a metallic thud. Frankie looked into the mirror and saw the bike and rider fall into the ditch. Jacob screamed. Frankie panicked and stepped on the gas.

"Frankie, you have to stop. You just hit someone. You have to go back. He might be hurt." Frankie picked up speed. "Please, Frankie," Jacob pleaded. "You're going to be in so much trouble if you don't go back."

Frankie tried to think about what he should do. If he went back, the guy could tell the cops that they hit him and left him. Jacob looked horrified as Frankie sped away.

"Frankie, stop, go back!"

The hard look in Frankie's eyes told him that pleading was useless. Frankie continued to his street, pulled into the drive, and looked at Jacob. Frankie's wild, panicked appearance scared him. He looked like an injured animal, and everyone knew an injured animal was dangerous.

"Don't you say a word, Wingate! You're just as guilty as I am. Remember, your dad's the preacher. What would he say or do to you if he found out? He'd probably send you away to reform school. It wouldn't make your dad look too good to have a son in trouble with the law." With that, Frankie opened the door and stepped out of the car. He glared at Jacob before he slammed the door and disappeared into the house.

Jacob leaned his head back against the seat. How could everything have gone so wrong? His dad would kill him. He thought for a minute and knew he couldn't tell him. Someone needed to know what had happened, but who could he tell? If he said anything, he was sure Frankie would make good on his threat. If only they hadn't moved to Florida.

CHAPTER
20

Jacob continued to drive Tanya to school. She could tell something was wrong between Frankie and Jacob. The only time they talked was at the dinner table, where they tried to pretend everything was okay. There was so much tension everyone felt it. Mr. and Mrs. Bonita were afraid to interfere. They didn't know where to begin.

Frankie had been parking his car on the side of the house, giving Jacob his spot. His dad had not said anything about the dent in his car. Frankie hoped he hadn't seen it. As they sat down to dinner that night, Frankie's dad asked about it. "I came out the other day and found a dent in your car. It looks like someone backed into it and left." Jacob dropped his fork. He turned pale.

"Jacob," Mrs. Bonita said, "are you all right?" Jacob looked at her in panic. Then, he looked at Frankie. Jacob saw the quick flash in his eyes.

"I ate something today, and I've had an upset stomach all day. Would you mind if I went and lay down for a while?" He excused himself and left the room. Frankie tried to lighten the mood.

"It was probably that nasty pizza they serve for lunch," he said. I'll check on him in a while.

Tanya helped clear the table, then went to find Jacob. He assured her he was fine. Tanya didn't believe him but let the subject drop.

The next day was horrible for Frankie. With all the pressure he was under, it was a miracle he hadn't cracked sooner. Mr. Fugate came into the classroom and saw Frankie sitting there. The other students had not yet arrived. "Well, Frankie, how's my favorite spic doing?" Frankie decided not to answer. "Why are you still here? You know I'm not going to pass you. There's no way I would give up anything to the likes of you." Frankie could feel his stomach gurgling. He wanted to get up and leave. In truth, he wanted to get up and punch Mr. Fugate. There was no way he could do either. If he left, then, Mr. Fugate would consider it a victory. If he hit him, then, he would be in Mr. Grimhold's office. There was no way he would allow that to happen.

As the class came in and took their seats, Mr. Fugate looked at Frankie and laughed. He knew he was beginning to crack Frankie's shell. It would only be a matter of time before he made Frankie so mad that he would lose control. He lived for that day. It was time for him to pay back the lowlife race that took his wife from him. It didn't matter that she said she'd left him because of his cruel and abusive attitude. He knew the real reason was Hispanic men like the one his wife ran off with were a no-good, lying set of thieves.

Frankie's mind continued to go back to the night of the accident. He was worried he would get caught. He feared more that he'd killed the person on the bicycle. Suddenly, Frankie found himself on the floor. He looked up at Mr. Fugate standing over him. "Thought you'd gone to sleep on me. Figured I'd better wake you up." Mr. Fugate had dumped him from his desk. Frankie picked himself up from the floor and sat back down in his seat. He looked around at the class. No one said a thing or laughed. They all sat, staring at their desks. "Don't look at them, Mr. Bonita, they aren't going to help you. They want to pass my class. They, at least, stand a chance."

Frankie began the assignment written on the board. He just had to get through the class this one day. Tomorrow, he would worry about the next day and the day after that. As he began to write, Mr. Fugate quietly slipped up the aisle behind Frankie. He knocked Frankie's backpack from the back of his seat. Frankie leaned down to pick it up. Mr. Fugate purposely tripped over Frankie and landed on the floor. The class began to laugh. "I'm so sorry, Mr. Fugate, I didn't see you there," Frankie said.

"Mr. Bonita, you have done it this time. I will see you expelled for your actions." He went to his desk and called for security. When the officer showed up, Mr. Fugate had Frankie removed from the classroom. "I'll be down after this period to speak with the principal about having him permanently removed from the school."

Frankie whirled around. "What? You're going to have me expelled because you knocked my backpack down and, then, tripped over it?" His voice began to rise, "Are you nuts?" He took a step toward Mr. Fugate and was grabbed by the officer. Mr. Fugate smiled as Frankie was removed from his classroom.

Frankie sat in the principal's office, waiting for his dad. He knew it didn't matter what he said; Mr. Fugate would win. His dad showed up and ordered him home. Frankie walked to his car. He squealed his tires as he pulled from the school parking lot. Instead of going home, he drove to the cabin. He walked the path through the woods, slowly listening to the sounds around him. Jacob was right; it was peaceful here. There were no problems out here. His thoughts returned to his day at school. He didn't know how he was going to handle this. He'd never had trouble until this year. All of his teachers liked him except for Mr. Fugate. What had he ever done to make Mr. Fugate hate him?

Frankie hated when he felt this way because he knew his thoughts would start turning dark. He pulled out a pin and began to prick his thigh. Before long, he began to scratch words into his skin. He saw the blood and the words *hate, useless, unfair*. The pricking and scratching began to calm him. He knew it made no sense. How could causing yourself pain have the opposite effect? He walked to a shelf in the corner and grabbed the bottle of alcohol. He cleaned the scratches and sat for a while longer. When the sun began to go down below the trees, he decided he needed to leave. He didn't want to walk through the woods in the dark since he hadn't brought a flashlight with him.

Frankie drove to his grandfather's house. If anyone listened to him, it would be his grandfather. When he pulled into his grandfather's drive, his grandfather was sitting outside.

"Popi," Frankie yelled. "How are you?"

His grandfather sat on the porch and said nothing. Frankie knew this was not a good sign. "Frankie, your dad is worried sick about you. He said you got kicked out of school, then didn't go home. What's going on?"

"I wish I knew what was going on. I have this teacher at school, and he has been after me all year. He is verbally abusive to me. Today, he purposely knocked my backpack off of my chair and, then, tripped over it. He told them I shoved him. He's accused me of cheating, lying, and stealing. He calls me greaser and other names. I'm not the only one he does this to in the class. He says things to all of the Hispanics in class." Frankie shifted from one foot to the other. He looked at the floor of the porch instead of at his grandfather. "I came to see if I could leave my car here. Every time I get in trouble, Dad takes my car and drives it. I know that he's mad that you gave the car to me and not to him. So can I keep it here?"

His grandfather looked at him. "Of course, you can keep it here." His grandfather sat back in his chair. "You know, Frankie, I was going to give the car to your dad. One day, I asked him to help me with something on the car. I needed to put a new engine in it. He said he was too busy. He wanted me to give him the car, but he didn't want to do any work on it. I tried to put the engine in by myself. The chain snapped, and I managed to move out of the way in time so that I didn't get hurt. However, I damaged the engine. Your dad was angry when he saw the engine was ruined, and he couldn't drive it. I felt he was so ungrateful that I decided right then and there he would never have the car. I'd sell it or give it away, but he would never drive it."

Frankie nodded his head. He understood what his grandfather had said. Frankie had come over when he was fifteen and helped his grandfather put the engine into the car. When he got his driver's license, his grandfather gave it to him as a birthday present. His dad was angry. He ruined his birthday party by yelling about how unfair it was that Frankie had received the car that should have been his. Whenever his dad was upset with him, the first thing he did was take away Frankie's car.

Frankie walked the mile and a half home from his grandfather's house. When he arrived, his dad was waiting for him. "Give me the keys to the car, Frankie." Frankie just looked at his dad. "Can't do it, Dad, I dropped the car and the keys off to Popi. I knew you'd take my car away without hearing my side of the story. I look at it this way, you don't want to believe in me or hear my side of the story. So I figure there's no reason you should have the pleasure of driving my car. I gave it back to Grandpa. After all, I pay him for the insurance because his name is the only other name on the title. Not yours." He stood tall as he spoke those words. He knew he was standing up for what was right, even if it came out as being rebellious. He no longer cared. It didn't matter what his dad did to him anymore. He no longer had any respect for him. He walked past his dad into the house and went straight to his room.

Frankie saw Tanya sitting on his bed. "I heard what happened. Several of the kids went to the office and told Mr. Grimhold what happened. Mr. Fugate gave them detention. He said you had bullied them into saying that."

Frankie looked at his sister. "It's okay, Tanya. I tried. I think God has given up on me because he sure is letting this happen to me. What I want to know is why." Frankie walked to his bed and sat on it. He rubbed the back of his neck. "No one can help me anymore, Tanya. I don't want you to worry about it."

Tanya smiled at her brother and gave him a hug. "Well, you're wrong about a lot of this. Your friends have continued to tape Mr. Fugate. After they had gotten in trouble for sticking up for you today, they called Mom. Two of them, John and Anthony, came over today while you were gone and gave mom the tapes they'd made. They also called Nathan's dad and talked with him because he's a lawyer. He called mom and talked with her for a long time. She's meeting with him tomorrow. They're going to sue the school board and the school." She bounced on the bed excitedly.

Frankie continued to sit still. "That's nice. Maybe it will keep the same thing from happening to someone else. I'm going to lie down, Tanya, so you need to leave my room." Frankie pushed himself up against the pillows. Tanya looked hurt as she stood up and walked out of the room, closing his door. She had never seen him this depressed before. What worried her more was what she had seen while sitting on the bed. She had seen fresh scratches on Frankie's legs. Maybe it was time she told her mom so that she could get him some help. She walked back to her own room and waited until she was called to dinner.

Frankie walked into the kitchen, expecting his dad to be there, but he was gone. "Hey, where's Dad? Did I make him so angry he doesn't want to eat with us?"

Frankie's mom looked at him, concerned. "No, Frankie, he went to talk to your grandfather about your car. It made him really mad that you defied him and left the car there." She began to wring her hands. "Frankie, while your dad is gone, I think it would be best if you ate and, then, went back to your room. That way, you'll be out of his sight when he returns." Frankie looked at his mom. She had large dark circles under her eyes and seemed to be stressed all of the time. He was afraid that it was all his fault.

Jacob sat, listening to this conversation. He was an outsider both here and at home. Because of Jacob's own dad, Frankie, and his family were having a difficult time. Jacob ate quietly and, then, offered to do the dishes. Mrs. Bonita was so tired from such a stressful day that she agreed to let him do them, as long as Tanya helped. Mrs. Bonita went to her room and lay down on the bed. She needed to get rid of the headache that she'd had most of the day. She knew how mad Frankie's dad was before he left, and she knew he would be even angrier when he returned.

Jacob entered Frankie's room quietly. "Frankie, can we talk?" Frankie didn't answer. "We really need to tell someone what happened." Frankie continued to lie in his bed. He refused to answer Jacob. "Frankie, I can't get it out of my head. I can't sleep anymore. My grades are dropping. You've been getting into more trouble, and now you've been kicked out of school. We have to tell someone. There was still no response from Frankie. If you won't tell someone, then, I will."

Frankie jumped to his feet and grabbed Jacob by the shirt. "You tell anyone, Jacob, and it will be the last thing you do. I will not go to jail because some idiot ran into my car. It was his fault." He shoved Jacob away from him and left his room, grabbing his backpack on his way out. Frankie slipped quietly into the kitchen, filling his backpack with peanut butter, bread, and a couple bottles of water. He grabbed a sleeping bag and a battery-powered lantern from the garage and walked down the drive. The cabin was only a short distance by foot. He could walk the two miles. If he saw headlights, he could always hide in the woods. Frankie figured it would be best if he stayed away from everyone for a few days.

Mr. Bonita returned to a dark house. He assumed everyone was in bed. His talk with his dad went the way it always did. He and his dad argued over Frankie's car. He was still bitter about his dad's decision to give it to Frankie. His dad's reply was always the same, "I didn't give it to him, Frankie earned it. He put all of the work into fixing it up that you were unwilling or too busy to do. That's why the car belongs to Frankie." The way Frankie had been behaving, he wouldn't be driving that car until he moved out. He'd show Frankie and his own father who was boss.

21

Jacob and Tanya sat silently, eating breakfast. Jacob watched Tanya chew her lower lip. They had heard the argument between Mr. Bonita and his wife when he returned home the night before.

Jacob knew from the argument that Mr. Bonita was angry with Frankie for leaving the car with his grandfather. Jacob wanted to leave before Tanya's parents were awake. They didn't bother knocking on Frankie's door since he wouldn't be going to school with them.

Jacob knew something was wrong by the end of the day. Kids were whispering in the hallway. There were cops and reporters inside and out. He was scared they had learned about the accident and was looking for Frankie. His fears intensified when he was called to the office. The secretary directed Jacob to a conference room next to the principal's office. He entered and sat at a long table. The conference table could have held up to fourteen people, but the only ones there were Jacob, Mrs. Bonita, and two men in suits.

Mrs. Bonita introduced Jacob to Nathan's father, Mr. Lewis, who was representing her and Frankie, and to Mr. Minsk from the school board. They asked him several questions about the happenings in Mr. Fugate's class. He admitted he had loaned his tape recorder to provide evidence of the bullying. Jacob was dismissed, and the next student was called in.

When Jacob and Tanya returned to her house that day, they sensed something was wrong long before they entered. They could hear Mr. Bonita yelling inside the house. They waited until things quieted down before they went inside. Mrs. Bonita sat on the couch, crying. Mr. Bonita came storming into the room. "Where is Frankie?" He looked at Tanya and Jacob. "Where are you two hiding him?" Tanya looked terrified.

"What do you mean where is Frankie? We've been in school all day. How would we know where he is?" Her father reached out and slapped her. Jacob jumped in front of her.

"No disrespect, Mr. Bonita, but that was uncalled for. We didn't see Frankie this morning when we ate breakfast, and we just now got home from school." Mr. Bonita clenched and unclenched his hands.

Tanya ran to her mother. "Mom, what's he talking about? What do you mean where's Frankie? Isn't he here?" They looked at Mr. Bonita as he laughed at them.

"How would your mom know? Instead of being an obedient wife and mother and staying here taking care of her duties, she was off causing trouble at school. You just can't let me handle this, can you?"

Mrs. Bonita had taken enough. She stood up and turned toward her husband. When she spoke, her voice was calm and steady. "That's the problem, Jose. You didn't handle it. You let some stranger mentally and physically abuse your own son. I spent the afternoon at the school listening to weeks of taped classes and watching videos of Mr. Fugate. I watched that man dump our son on the floor, slap him around, accuse him of cheating, and other horrible things because he's Hispanic. I learned his wife ran off with a Hispanic man, and Mr. Fugate was taking it out on all of the Hispanic boys. I met their mothers who thanked me for standing up for them. You're right, I wasn't here.

"I was where I was needed, doing the job you should have done to protect our son." She went to her bedroom, slamming the door behind her.

Mr. Bonita dropped on the couch, staring at the floor. "She's right. I tried to be a good father." He looked at Jacob. "I did exactly what your dad told me I needed to do." He put his head in his hands, and his shoulders began to shake. "I deserted my own son, and he's gone."

Jacob sat across from Mr. Bonita. "Just because you don't know where he is doesn't mean he's gone. Like all of us, sometimes, you just need to get away for a while. Sometimes we need to walk it off to clear our head. I'm sure he'll show up."

The front door opened, and Frankie walked in, looking around the living room. "What's wrong, is Mom, okay?" Tanya ran to him and hugged him. "Whoa, sis, what's all this about?" He watched the tears flow down her cheeks. He saw Jacob sitting next to his dad and assumed the worse.

Frankie's dad spoke first. "I thought you'd run away. I came home from work, and you were gone. Then, I received a call from the principal telling me your mom was at school with a lawyer. Mr. Fugate has been put on administrative leave while they investigate all the alleged abuse. You tried to tell me, and I wouldn't listen." Mr. Bonita looked at Jacob. "Instead, I chose to listen to Jacob's father. I figured, since he was our spiritual guide, that he would know what I should do. Instead, all I did was made things worse." He rubbed his hands together. "Can you forgive me, Frankie?"

Frankie knew he should say something to make his dad feel better. He had been hurt by his dad's disbelief for so long. He looked at his father, turned, and walked to his room without saying a word.

Mr. Bonita looked at Jacob. "I need to ask you a question. I'll understand if you don't want to answer me, and I won't think any less of you if you don't." He looked at the floor and swallowed hard. "Jacob, you've seen how I've been handling my family. I know it's completely different than the way I was when you first met me. Is the way I've been treating my family the way your dad treats you and your mom?"

Jacob thought before he answered. "I love my dad. I know he wants what is best for everyone. However, I think he goes overboard. Yes, this is how he treats us. I think he feels inadequate, at times, but I don't know why. His dad was a preacher and didn't treat his family this way. When my dad feels like he's losing control at home, he usu-ally gives his rebellion sermon at church. It causes quite a stir for a while. No one sees my dad treat us that way. It's all done in private." Jacob stood up and walked across the room and looked out the front window.

Mr. Bonita came up behind Jacob and put his hand on his shoulder. "Frankie and Tanya told me about the move and your friend. He really didn't tell you anything?"

Jacob looked at Mr. Bonita. His voice had an edge to it when he spoke. "Nope, not a thing. I learned we were moving the day before we left and learned about my friend after we got down here. I learned about their trip to the Holy Land the same time Frankie and Tanya did."

Mr. Bonita shook his head. "You know, my wife made a comment the other day about me turning into the person I used to be. I didn't want to believe it, but I see it now. I hope my family can forgive me. I especially hope you can forgive me, Jacob."

Jacob looked surprised. "What do I need to forgive you for?"

Mr. Bonita grabbed Jacob and hugged him. "For acting just like your father. It must be difficult to love someone who treats you like that. I did the same thing to you, and I am so sorry." Jacob looked into Mr. Bonita's tear-filled eyes and nodded.

"Not a problem, Mr. B. I forgive you." He walked over and sat next to Tanya. "I guess, I'd best get my things packed. I'm just waiting for my parents to call and tell me they are home. Their flight should've been in about an hour ago." He stood and went to Frankie's room to pack. When he entered, Frankie picked up a book and refused to look at Jacob.

"You know what, Frankie? You really should give your dad a second chance. You never know when you'll need him to stick by your side and support you." He grabbed his bags and sat in his car, waiting for the call.

22

At dinner, Jacob's mother could not be quiet about all of the wonders she had seen. For years, she had wished to visit the Holy Land for as long as Jacob could remember. "Jacob, we spent our first night eating dinner along the Mediterranean Sea. We visited the Roman amphitheater and aqueduct and ate dinner in Abraham's tent. All of this was a reenactment of that time. We wore costumes and ate authentic food. We visited the Garden of Gethsemane. You could feel the sorrow and pressure that Christ must have felt that night as he prayed. It's a beautiful and peaceful area. Finally, we saw the house where Jesus was beaten, and then, we visited the tomb where we had communion." She took a deep breath. "I'll remember this trip until the day I take my last breath."

Jacob could tell it had been a very personal and spiritual trip for his mom. Her face glowed. He looked at his dad and waited for him to speak. "Yes, it was very moving. This was my fifth trip with members of the church, so I made sure they saw all the usual places. I guess, when you've been there as many times as I've been there, it just isn't all that special anymore."

Jacob was shocked. His dad continued to eat as if the trip was nothing more than a boring vacation. Jacob looked at his mom. "I imagine when I finally get to go, I'll feel just like you. To think, you were walking where the disciples and Jesus walked and where he died. It would bring it all so much closer home."

Jacob heard a snort from his dad. "Didn't you mean to say, 'if you ever get to go,' instead of when you get to go? The rate your grades are going, the only place you will be going is to a local grocery store to work. The first thing I did when I got home was checked your grades." Jacob sighed and shut his mouth. It was just like his dad to ruin the moment. It was almost as if he didn't want anyone else to be happy. Jacob knew his mom was tired, so he volunteered to clean the kitchen for her.

It was nine o'clock when Tanya called. He could tell she'd been crying. "Jacob, Frankie is gone again. He and Dad had an argument. Dad tried to apologize, and Frankie told him off and walked out of the house. He's getting so moody and hateful anymore. I'm scared. Something is wrong. Has he talked to you lately? Do you know what's happening?" Jacob knew exactly what was happening. He just couldn't tell Tanya.

"Try to get some rest, Tanya, we'll talk about this at school tomorrow." He hung up the phone and knew that he was not going to be able to sleep. He knew what was wrong, and until he found a way to solve it, he would continue to lie awake each night.

Jacob got up early the next morning. He didn't expect to see his mother sitting in the Florida room this early. "Good morning, Jacob. Did I wake you?" she asked. Jacob shook his head no and poured himself a cup of coffee. He sat opposite his mother. She seemed to be in a contemplative mood. He had not seen her like this in years. There was peace in her face. It reminded him of the Christmas cards they would sometimes get with the image of Madonna on it. "So tell me how things went while I was gone."

Jacob decided to tell her only a little of what had happened. He was sure they would hear more later. He told her what Frankie's mom had done. He told her about the abuse of other Hispanic kids by Mr. Fugate and how much it had affected Frankie. What he didn't tell her was how much trouble his dad had caused or that he was in trouble and didn't know what to do about the accident. He was going to have to tell someone before long because it was beginning to eat him up inside.

Tanya was waiting outside when Jacob pulled up. There were dark circles under her red eyes. "Have you heard anything from Frankie?" She shook her head. She obviously didn't want to talk about it. "Well, then, we'll just pray about it. Before they pulled out of the drive, Jacob turned to Tanya, took her hand, and prayed for Frankie's safety. He prayed Frankie would find peace and an answer to what was bothering him. They pulled out and headed to school. They had only gone about a mile when they saw Frankie walking toward the house. Jacob started to pull over, and Frankie waved them away. He definitely didn't want to talk to them, no matter what.

Tanya and Jacob could feel a difference in the atmosphere at school. There seemed to be more parents there than usual. Most of them were Hispanic. He was sure that the word had just gotten out about Mr. Fugate. Jacob wondered why more parents had not come forward sooner. He asked one of his classmates that question and was shocked to learn that many of the Hispanic parents were illegal aliens and afraid to cause any trouble. Their kids always behaved for fear they would be caught and deported. It was tough because most of the kids were born in the United States. In Jacob's mind, Florida was a very complicated place to live.

He managed to make it through the rest of the day without any problems. When Jacob met Tanya at the car, she seemed like she was in a better mood. Maybe if he told her what had happened, then, she would know what to do. Perhaps, she would be able to talk with Frankie about the situation. Frankie definitely wouldn't listen to him anymore.

Jacob called his mom and asked if she would call Tanya's parents. They were going to go to the mall and would be home by dinner. At the mall, they walked to the food court and ordered sodas and fries, then sat at a corner table away from everyone. Jacob decided it was time to get the burden off of his chest. He told Tanya about the night of the accident. She had known something was wrong. She knew there had to be more to Frankie's mood than just Mr. Fugate. They sat and discussed different options.

"Jacob, let me call my brother and see if he'll listen to me. I don't want to call in here because there's no privacy." Jacob and Tanya drove to a small park not far from the mall. They sat on a picnic table, and Tanya called her brother.

"Frankie, listen, I need to talk to you. Jacob and I are concerned about you. He told me about the accident." She could hear him swear under his breath. "Frankie, we need to figure out what to do about this. It isn't going to go away. There has to be a way to fix this—to make it right." There was silence on the other end. She thought maybe he had laid the phone down.

"Okay, Tanya. Put the bonehead on and let me talk to him." Tanya handed the phone to Jacob. "Listen, Jacob, I don't appreciate you telling my sister about the accident. Now you've dragged her into it as well. But now that you have, I guess I don't have a choice. We need to sit and figure this out. I can't keep going like this. After dinner tomorrow, why don't you pick my sister up like you're going on a date. Meet me at the cabin. I'll have her drive my car home, and we can take your car down to the police station. We'll let Tanya tell our parents when she returns. That way, they can get things going. You know, find a lawyer, pray, decide whether they're going to kill us or not." Frankie laughed, trying to make it sound like a joke. He knew his parents probably would be close to killing him. "Hey, you can bring some snacks. I've got a bottle of soda here, and I'll bring out a pizza. Might as well have one last meal. Tell Tanya I'll be home in about an hour." Frankie hung up the phone, unaware of the shadow that slipped quietly back into the woods. He had no way of knowing someone had followed him and overheard his conversation

Frankie sat at the table in full panic mode. He had read stories about people who had hit someone and left the scene. He'd be thrown in prison for the rest of his life. He had to convince Jacob and his sister not to say anything. He needed more time to figure this out. His head had been pounding for several hours. Frankie looked in his backpack for the bottle of aspirin he always kept with him. What he pulled out was not his aspirin but a bottle of Xanax from his medicine cabinet. His mom had taken him to a psychiatrist back when he was suffering from anxiety. They had given him the Xanax to help relieve the symptoms. He hated how drowsy they made him feel. A thought came to him. It would be so easy to take the whole bottle and just go to sleep and never wake up. That kind of thinking scared him. He grabbed the bottle off the table and threw them out the door into the woods. No sense in having the temptation around. He checked the cabin, grabbed his backpack, and started the walk home. He couldn't wait to get his car tomorrow.

Mr. Fugate watched Frankie pass through the trees. He couldn't believe his luck. He'd been on his way home when he saw Frankie duck into the woods. He parked his car up the road, then silently followed the path. He walked as silent as possible, and then, he saw the cabin in the woods. What luck. He waited for it to get darker before approaching. He could see Frankie sitting at a table inside, through one of the windows. He ducked down when he heard Frankie's phone ring. He listened to Frankie's side of the conversation and knew he had him. There had been some kind of accident, and Frankie was responsible. He would see him in jail if it was the last thing he did. Mr. Fugate slid back into the woods and waited for Frankie to leave. It wasn't long before he heard him walking up the path past him. He waited ten minutes to make sure Frankie didn't return before he slipped down to the cabin. His foot kicked something on the ground, and its rattling sound made him pick it up. The door had been padlocked. He carefully and quietly walked around the cabin. When he tried the French doors, he found them unlocked. He slipped inside and shined his flashlight around. Inside, he found an ice chest with half a bottle of soda. He looked at the bottle of pills he had picked up and the bottle of soda and a plan began to form in his mind.

CHAPTER

23

Tension at school the next day was high. Everyone was talking about Mr. Fugate and Frankie. Tanya and Jacob refused to comment. They would leave all of that mess to the adults. They had enough to think about. Tanya was still worried about her brother. Jacob was afraid he would go to jail along with Frankie. They managed to make it through the day without too many people bothering them. Jacob dropped Tanya at her door, promising to come back for her in a couple of hours. He drove home and went straight to his room. He tried to read but couldn't concentrate.

Jacob looked at his clock and saw that it was almost six o'clock. He walked into the living room where his mom and dad were reading. "I'm headed over to Tanya's house, we're going to the movies. See you later." Jacob's father continued reading. His mom looked up at him and smiled.

"Have a nice time, honey, and drive safe. I love you." She looked back down at her book. Jacob walked out of the house to his car and drove slowly to Tanya's house. The evening was cool. Even though it was spring, it was evident that winter was still trying to hold on. Florida had the craziest weather. It could be in the eighties during the day and in the low sixties in the evenings. Jacob pulled into Tanya's drive and glanced into the back seat to make sure he had his jacket. He thought about what he would say to Frankie as he walked to the door and rang the bell. Tanya's mom opened the door and invited him in. He followed Mrs. Bonita into the living room and sat on the couch across from Mr. Bonita.

Mr. Bonita was talking to Jacob about school when Tanya walked in. Jacob looked at her. "Wow! You look great!" She wore no makeup but needed none. Her beauty was all natural. She had on a simple short-sleeved shirt and a pair of jeans. "Hey, Tanya, you might want to grab a jacket. The theater usually gets a little chilly, and if the temperature drops like it did last night, you'll definitely need it." Tanya went back to her room to get a light jacket. When she returned, she kissed her mom and dad goodbye.

"Night, Mom and Dad, I love you." She and Jacob walked out to the car. He held the door for her like his mom and dad had trained him to do. As he put on his seatbelt, he thought about the lie he had told his parents. This was something he seldom did. He couldn't tell them where he was really going. He didn't want them to know about Frankie's hidden cabin. Jacob drove to the nearest convenience store. He grabbed a bag of chips and some donuts. He thought it would be smart to have something salty and sweet. Besides, if they ended up in jail, who knew how long it would be before they could have their favorite snacks.

Jacob had never driven to the cabin by himself, so he followed Tanya's directions. It was funny to think how close the cabin was to Frankie's house, and no one seemed to know about it. Frankie had pulled off to the side as far as he could so Jacob could pull his car in as far as possible. With its green color, it blended in with the trees. Jacob and Tanya grabbed the snacks and their jackets. It was always cooler near the water. Frankie stood on the porch, waiting apprehensively for Jacob and his sister. He saw them walking through the woods and took a deep breath. He had to find a way to convince Jacob to wait a little longer.

"About time you got here," Frankie joked. "Got the snacks?" Jacob held up the two bags as he followed Frankie into the cabin. "Coke okay?" Frankie asked. "That's all I got."

Tanya sat at the table, drumming her fingers. "Coke is fine, Frankie." She was worried about her brother and Jacob. Frankie handed his sister and Jacob a cup of soda.

"Good job, Frankie, what'd you do chill the bottle?" Jacob asked as he took another sip.

"I figured it might be a long time before we have a cold soda again, so yeah, that's exactly what I did. I put it in the cooler last night after I drank the first half. I also put your cups in there. I know they're only plastic but figured it couldn't hurt." Frankie realized he was rambling. He ran his hand through his hair and sat down. He opened the box of pizza and put a slice on each plate. Then, he reached for a donut. "Cool, you brought chocolate glazed. Did Tanya tell you that they're my favorite?" Frankie looked from his sister to Jacob.

Jacob grabbed a chocolate-glazed donut for himself and looked at Frankie with a grin. "They can't be your favorite because they're mine." He bit into the sweet, sticky donut and smiled a chocolate smile at Tanya. She laughed at him as she nibbled at the edges of a plain glazed donut. The air was tense. Jacob didn't know how to start the conversation with Frankie. This was a conversation he didn't want to rush into. He was afraid it would push Frankie over the edge. They began to nibble at their pizza and drank their soda in silence. Jacob yawned and looked at Tanya who was also yawning.

Frankie smiled at the two of them. "Hey, what's wrong? Am I that boring?" Frankie joked and, then, found himself yawning. He refilled their cups with soda.

Jacob shook his head to clear it. "No, I think I've been under so much stress that I'm just now feeling the weight lift off of me. It has been a pretty heavy weight." He lifted his cup of soda and drank it down.

Frankie lowered his head and frowned. "I know. I don't think anyone has been as stressed as me." He stood and walked to the open window. "I feel like I've let everyone down. I've made a mess of this year."

Tanya stood up and walked to her brother. "No, Frankie, you haven't. Dad should have listened to you. If he had, then, Mr. Fugate would not have been able to torment you the way he had." She felt light-headed and fell against her brother. He grabbed hold of her.

"Whoa. You okay, Tanya?"

She held onto him tighter. "Yeah, I just feel real dizzy."

Frankie looked down at her. Did you eat anything besides that slice of pizza today? Maybe your sugar is low or something." He helped her back to the table and got her soda. Jacob looked like he could fall asleep any minute.

Frankie handed Tanya her soda and watched while she finished it. He looked up and saw Jacob with his head on the table, sound asleep. "Tanya, you know this is all my fault. I made this mess and got Jacob caught up in it. None of it was his fault. I don't want you to wake Jacob until I'm gone."

Tanya felt the panic rising. "What are you going to do, Frankie?"

Frankie loved how concerned his sister was. He loved her so much. That's why he had to protect her and her boyfriend. "I'm going to go home, tell Mom and Dad, and have them drive me to the police station. That way, I'll leave Jacob out of this. Give me about a half hour, and then, wake lover boy up and tell him." He stood, grabbed his soda, kissed Tanya on the head, and walked out the door. Tanya lay her head on the table and cried. She was so proud of her brother, but she was scared for him too. She cried until she fell asleep.

Mr. Fugate watched Frankie leave the cabin. This was working out better than he had hoped. He slipped into the cabin and found Tanya and Jacob asleep at the table, their cups empty.

Mr. Fugate slid the cot across the room and against the wall. He laid Frankie's sleeping bag on top of it. Gently, he lifted Tanya up and placed her in a sitting position on the cot. He put a pillow between her head and the wall. He looked at the manacles hanging on the wall. He looked through Frankie's gym bag until he found a shirt that he tore into strips. He wrapped the pieces around the rusty metal. Then, he placed one manacle around Tanya's right ankle. He grabbed Jacob under the arms and dragged him to the cot and put him next to Tanya. He removed Jacob's jacket and proceeded to fasten his left ankle in the manacle. Then, he covered them with their Jackets. Next, he moved the table close enough they could get to it. He replaced the bottle of soda with an untainted bottle and slid it and the donuts within their reach. He moved the ice chest closer to them. Inside, he placed four small bottles of water.

He was unsure of how long they would sleep. He left a flashlight on the table in case it was still dark when they woke up. Then, he made sure he removed the battery from their cell phones. He placed the batteries into his pocket. He'd get rid of them later. He didn't want them to call anyone until he was sure Frankie was in jail. He had to pay for what he and his kind had done to him. Mr. Fugate walked around the shack, locking up the shutters. He didn't want any creatures coming in on them. He wasn't sure what kind of animals might be out here in the woods, but he was not going to make the kids food for them. His problem was with Frankie, not these two. He locked the padlock on the cabin door, walked to his car, and drove home.

Frankie parked his car in the drive. When he entered the house, the lights were off. His parents were in bed, so he went to his room and sat on the bed. He downed the rest of his soda, figuring the best thing he could do was take a shower, change clothes, and then, wake his parents. He lay back on his bed to stretch and rest for a minute and slid into a deep and dreamless sleep.

24

Frankie was jarred awake by a commotion in the kitchen that sounded like someone was crying. He could hear other voices in the house. He tried to stand and found his head swimming. He sat back for a moment until he felt he could stand without passing out. He had not moved all night, so why was he so drowsy? His head felt full and fuzzy. What had he done the night before to feel this way? He looked at his dresser and saw his soda cup and knew he had not been drinking alcohol. He walked down the hallway. As he reached the entrance to the living room, he saw his dad hugging his mom. Tears streamed down her face. Mr. and Mrs. Wingate sat on the other couch, and across from them was an officer. Frankie's blood ran cold. He couldn't move into the living room.

Mrs. Bonita looked up and saw the concern on her son's face and motioned him in. He looked around at everyone.

"What's going on? Why are the police here?" He surveyed the room. "Where's Tanya?"

This question brought a fresh outburst from his mom.

"Mom, you're scaring me," Frankie said. "Where's Tanya? Is she okay? Is she in the hospital? Will someone please answer me?" Frankie's voice had reached a high-pitched panic.

Mr. Wingate was the first to speak. "We don't know where your sister is, Frankie. For that matter, we don't know where Jacob is either."

Frankie clenched his fists. "What do you mean you don't know where Jacob is?"

Mr. Wingate stood up and moved toward Frankie. Frankie instinctively took a step back. "Jacob picked your sister up last night to go to a movie. No one has seen them since they left. We've checked with the theater, and no one recognized their picture."

Frankie stumbled backward and dropped into the chair. How could his sister be missing? "Have you checked the creeks and rivers around here? People who don't know the area are always making wrong turns and running off of boat ramps." He spoke quicker and louder. "Have you tried her phone? Her phone is always on. She's on that thing like twenty-four seven. Have you checked with her friends? What did they say? He realized he was speaking too fast."

Mr. Bonita walked to his son and knelt down in front of him. He grabbed him by the shoulders and shook him. "Frankie, you've got to stop. You're terrifying your mother." Frankie looked up at his dad. Mr. Bonita could see his son breaking inside. He grabbed him and hugged him to his chest. Together, the two of them sobbed. Frankie pushed himself back and wiped his eyes with the back of his hands.

"Dad, we've got to do something. I can't just sit here. What can I do?"

Mr. Bonita looked at his son. "We've checked your sister's room. We've come up with a list of names of people she knows or is friends with. Why don't you contact them and see if any of them have seen her or heard from her?" He led Frankie over to the officer. He felt uncomfortable being this close to the law. However, he needed to help find his sister. He hoped she was okay. Was she scared? Was she in danger or dead? The officer handed him a list of names with phone numbers. Frankie went to his room and began to call all of Tanya's friends. After each call, he slammed his fist down on his desk. It was frustrating. The more calls he made, the more frustrated and angry he became. How was it possible, in an area as small as Strawberry Ridge, that no one had seen Jacob or Tanya? Frankie's mind began to wander. Had Tanya run away with Jacob? Why would they do such a thing? He knew that Mr. Wingate could be overbearing at times but not enough to chase Jacob out of his home. If he did run away, did he force Tanya to go with him, or did she go willingly?

Frankie called the last two names on the list. Neither one of them had seen his sister. He took the list back into the living room. He glanced out his front window and could see the news crew setting up out front. He walked to his dad and asked him about it and was told that they would be speaking with the press in the next few minutes. Frankie felt as if he had been punched in the gut. The newscast made it all seem too real. He racked his brain. Had Tanya said anything to him yesterday that might tell him where she was? He remembered talking to Tanya and Jacob and eating pizza and donuts. After that, his mind was blank. He didn't remember driving home or going to bed.

Frankie sat in the living room with the television turned to the newscast happening in his own front yard. His parents were pleading for the return of their young daughter. He could see the strain and tears on his mom's face. The Wingate's stepped up to the microphone. They held up a picture of their son and pleaded for any information. They clung to each other, afraid to let go, literally holding each other up.

By that evening, the house was full of people. There were kids everywhere. They were trying to figure out what had happened to Jacob and Tanya. It didn't seem like it would be in their nature to run off. No one had any fresh ideas. Both Tanya and Jacob were considered dedicated and responsible students. They would be the least likely couple to run off together. They hadn't known each other very long.

Frankie walked out the back door to get some fresh air. The food had been pouring in all day. There was more food than they had space. No one really felt like eating anything. Frankie's family was feeding off of the strength of those around them. He walked to the end of the dock and sat in one of the chairs. He looked at the seat his sister usually sat in. He absently rubbed his hand on the arm of the chair. His thoughts went back to when they had first moved into this house.

Tanya was only a year younger than Frankie. She had always looked up to him to protect her. They would sit on the edge of the dock, and he would pretend he was going to shove her in and let the alligators eat her. The truth was she wasn't scared of the alligators. She loved watching them glide through the water.

Frankie remembered the first time they'd held a picnic at the end of the dock. It was just the two of them. He had been reading a book, and Tanya had gone inside to get them something cool to drink. She had been gone for a long time. He figured she had gotten sidetracked and was getting ready to go in to get his own drink. That was when Tanya showed up with the picnic basket. She had two bottles of ice-cold soda, and two peanut-butter-and-jelly sandwiches. She had decided they would have a picnic.

As Frankie sat remembering these events, he smiled. His sister was so loving and caring. He couldn't imagine what kind of monster had his sister. He didn't want to think about how scared she might be. He buried his head in his hands. His body shook as the reality sunk in. If they didn't get a clue soon, then, he might never see his sister again.

Frankie never heard the footsteps on the dock. He felt a hand on his shoulder. He recognized the feel of that hand. His father stood behind him. "Frankie, how are you holding up?"

Frankie lifted his tear-stained face up toward his father and shook his head. There was no sense in lying to him. He knew if he tried to convince his parents that he was keeping it all together, they would see through it. He stood and grabbed his dad in a hug and cried. He clung to him and cried like he had when he was a small child and lost his first pet. When Frankie had cried it all out, he walked with his dad to the house. He remembered Jacob's words about forgiving his dad because he might need his support, one day. He felt humbled and ashamed. "Dad, I'm sorry I didn't tell you the other day that I forgive you. I hope you'll forgive me for the way I've been acting lately." His dad hugged him tighter, nodded, but said nothing. Frankie figured his dad was trying as hard as he was, just to hold it all together.

Around seven o'clock in the evening, people from the church started going home. The Bonitas were left with the Wingates and the void they all felt without their children. Mr. and Mrs. Bonita offered their guest room to the preacher and his wife. The Wingate's turned it down. It was vital that they get home in case someone called them about Jacob. Both families knew it was going to be one of the longest nights of their life. Frankie watched both sets of parents. He felt fuzzy-headed like he should remember something. He just couldn't think what it was.

25

Tanya was the first to wake up. Her body felt stiff and cold. It was light outside. She could see the sun shining on the water through the French doors of the small shack. What she couldn't figure out was why she couldn't move. Her head felt fuzzy and full. She heard a snore and realized Jacob was beside her. She shook him until he woke up.

Jacob looked around. His head felt full of mud. "Tanya, what time is it?"

Tanya looked at her watch. "It's 7:30 in the morning. Mom is going to ground me when she finds out I didn't come home last night. Then, she's going to kill me when she finds out I spent the night out here with you."

Jacob tried to get up from the cot. His left leg was asleep. He assumed he had slept crooked on the leg but was shocked to find out he was chained to the wall. He looked at Tanya and saw the panicked look in her eyes when she realized she was also chained. They looked around the cabin. Things had been moved around. The table had been moved from the center of the room to in front of the cot. They had drinks and snacks and the cooler. Something became urgently obvious. There was no bathroom and no way they were going to be able to hold it.

Jacob looked around the room. He spotted a small bucket. It was close enough; his toe touched it. He managed to slide it close to them. Jacob took the sleeping bag from the cot and held it up between them. This allowed Tanya a small amount of privacy. When she was finished, she did the same for Jacob. The bucket slid under the bed. Jacob found an empty pizza box to sit on top of the bucket. He hoped it would keep the smell down. He looked at the table. There were just a few snacks. He didn't know how long it would be before someone came for them. He wasn't sure if anyone would, but he didn't want to tell Tanya. He felt sure whoever had done this to them would be back soon.

The mosquitoes were able to squeeze through every crack in the shack. Jacob and Tanya seemed to be the feast of the day.

Jacob tried to figure out precisely what had happened. He remembered eating a donut, some pizza, and drinking some soda, and feeling tired. He assumed it was from the sugar. "Tanya, this may sound stupid but any idea of how we ended up like this? I remember the donut, pizza, and soda, feeling tired, then nothing until we woke up."

Tanya looked at Jacob, perplexed. She had an idea, but it was too horrible to think about. Jacob saw the hesitation. "Tanya, you don't really think Frankie had anything to do with this, do you?" Tanya didn't reply. If she opened her mouth to speak, she knew she'd start crying.

Jacob was silent for a minute. "Why, Tanya? Why would he do such a thing? Did he consider us such a threat that he would chain us in a cabin?"

A river of tears began to flow down Tanya's face again. "Jacob, what do you think his intentions are? Do you think he was planning to leave us here to die?"

Jacob grabbed Tanya's hand and rubbed the back of it. "No, I'm sure he's trying to figure out how to keep us quiet. I don't think he plans to harm us." Those very thoughts had been going through his mind, but he refused to voice them. "Did he say anything to you last night before he left?"

Tanya thought hard. She remembered talking with Frankie but couldn't remember what he'd said. She was frustrated. Why couldn't she remember? She shook her head.

"I think we need to ration things until we find out what's going on," Jacob said. "There is no telling how long it will be before whoever chained us up will be back to give us more water or food. If we can hang in until then, we'll find out why they're holding us here. I'm sure, it is all a misunderstanding."

Tanya looked at Jacob. "I think it was Frankie. He's been depressed lately. I know he's been harming himself again. I've seen the bloody tissues and the scratches on his leg. I think he's been under so much stress lately that when I called him yesterday, he panicked."

Jacob looked at Tanya with raised eyebrows. A chill went down his spine. Could it really be true? "Hey, Tanya, how many times have you been out here to the shack?"

Tanya brushed a piece of hair from her eyes. "I've been out here two or three times. There really wasn't anything for me to do out here. Frankie liked to come out here to relax. Sitting at the water's edge, watching nature always relaxed him. When I was little, he would hold my hand and take me to the end of the dock and tell me stories about the different animals we would see. He told me a story about this large alligator we had that used to watch us from the other side of the river. He called him the Swamp King and would make up all of these adventures for him."

Jacob watched the far-off look in Tanya's face. He could tell that she was reliving some special memories. "You really look up to your brother, don't you?" Jacob asked.

Tanya tried to reposition herself on the small cot so that she was facing Jacob and sitting with her legs crossed, Indian style. She smiled as she answered him. "He was always there when my parents were having problems. When my dad used to drink, he would get outraged over everything. He and my mom would scream and yell, and Frankie would come into my room and sit with me or take me for walks outside. He knew how to slip out of the house so my dad wouldn't see us." Tanya lowered her head and spoke softly. "He always protected me. There were a few times when Frankie tried to stand up to my dad to protect my mom. My dad would smack him around. One time, I ran in, crying, to grab hold of my mom. My dad jerked me away, and I fell down. My dad came toward me. I don't know if he was going to hit me or help me up. Frankie jumped between us. This made my dad so mad he started beating Frankie. My mom tried to intervene, and Frankie shoved her away. He took a beating for both of us."

Jacob had to ask the question that had been nagging him. "I can understand Frankie holding me here because I knew about the accident. I was with him. What I don't understand is if he always protected you, why he would do this to you? From what you just told me, I can't believe it is him. But if it isn't him, then, who would do this?"

Tanya was silent for a minute before she answered. "If it is Frankie, he would do this for survival. Frankie's in survival mode and can't see any way out of the situation. Maybe he's doing what he has to do to survive. I think he left us here until he can get a clear idea in his head of what he wants to do to make this situation right."

The mood was beginning to become dark and somber, so Jacob tried to lighten it. "Well, I can understand his panic. I just hope he figures it out before our portable toilet gets full. We have no place and no way of dumping it." Jacob laughed at his own joke, and Tanya slowly laughed along with him.

CHAPTER 26

Frankie pulled out a notebook and started writing down all of the things they had done that day. When had he last seen Tanya and Jacob? He remembered having a phone conversation with Tanya, and she said something about a movie. He remembered they had eaten pizza and had sodas at the cabin. That was before the movie. Where could they have gone? The police had been out all day, looking for Jacob's car. Frankie laughed to himself. There was no way the police could miss a car that was painted such a garish-green.

The sun began to set. Frankie was so exhausted he decided to go to bed early. The police told them they would return early in the morning to discuss other options for finding Tanya and Jacob. Frankie got the idea that the police thought the two of them had run off together. Tanya was too level-headed to try something like that. Frankie knew her well enough to know if she was going to run away with Jacob, she would have confided in him. They kept very few secrets from each other. As he drifted off to sleep, his mind thought about the secrets he had been keeping. Suddenly, it was as if his brain had hit a wall. He couldn't think of a single secret. Maybe he really had changed, and his secret-keeping days were over. Frankie heard his parents enter their bedroom. He heard them mention Tanya's name before he closed his eyes.

Mr. and Mrs. Bonita were worried about Tanya and Jacob. It had been over twenty-four hours since they had last seen them. They didn't know what else to do but to pray for their safekeeping. Mr. Bonita had another worry on his mind. It had been several years since he had seen Frankie fall apart the way he had earlier in the day. The last time Frankie had hugged him so tight was the night he told Frankie he was under a doctor's care and was going to join Alcoholics Anonymous. Frankie had carried the burden of being the man of the house for so long. It was a relief to Frankie to have his dad take over that role. Tonight, there seemed to be so much more to Frankie's emotions. But Mr. Bonita was unable to figure out what was bothering him. As he turned off the light, he could hear his wife crying softly. He turned to her, rubbing her back. "We'll find them, and they'll be okay. We just have to trust God on this." He felt his wife settle a little. He knew sleep was not going to come quickly. Mr. Bonita slid out of bed and walked to the living room. As he neared the couch, he fell to his knees and sobbed silently into the cushions. He prayed, asking God to protect both of his children and Jacob. He begged God to help him find them. He paused in his prayer, afraid to pray the next thing on his mind. He prayed and asked God to help him accept whatever the outcome was. He prayed for the strength to be the leader and broad shoulders of the family. He prayed for God to give him the power to forgive the person who had taken his daughter away.

As he lifted his head, he noticed a calm presence in the room. There was no one there that he could see. It was as if the place had been lit from within with a warmth that could only be described as unconditional love. He felt at peace with whatever would happen next. Suddenly, his body felt exhausted. He walked back to his bedroom and slid into bed. He was asleep almost as soon as his head hit the pillow. The strange glow from the living room permeated the bedroom, bringing peace with it.

Frankie tossed and turned in his bed, dreaming he was running from something or someone. In his dream, he could hear Jacob and Tanya calling to him. He was powerless to help them. He couldn't help himself. His muscles began to tire. His brain seemed to slow down, but he didn't know which way to go. He stopped, looking around him, there was nothing but darkness and confusion. He could hear metal scraping metal and Jacob screaming. He dropped to his knees, his head in his hands, and rocked back-and-forth, trying to hide from whatever was coming for him. He tried to block out Tanya and Jacob's screams. He rocked back-and-forth until he had rocked himself out of his bed and onto his floor.

Frankie sat in the darkness. There was something he needed to do. Only he could help Tanya and Jacob, but he didn't know how. His pajamas were soaked with his sweat. He undressed and took a shower. He hoped that the cleansing water would have the same effect on his mind that it had on his body because he needed to relax. He looked down at his thighs. He had started to scratch deeper and deeper. It seemed like it took longer and more pressure for him to find the relief.

Frankie walked out of the shower with a towel wrapped around his waist and sat on the edge of his bed. He looked at his nightstand and the pin that lay there. He dipped the end in alcohol and wiped it on a tissue. He brought the tip to his thigh. As the tip touched his skin, he closed his eyes. He applied a small amount of pressure. When that didn't work, he pushed harder. He felt the stab of pain and the relief that came with it. He let his mind and the pain take over. Only when the pressure was gone and he felt wholly relieved did he open his eyes. He grabbed the bottle of peroxide and the bottle of alcohol. He cleaned the scratches with the peroxide, watching the tiny white bubble form along the cut lines. As he looked, he noticed a word forming. "Evil" is what it said. Why would he subconsciously cut the word evil into his leg? Was he evil? Maybe he was evil, and that was why Tanya was missing. He wiped away the peroxide foam and soaked a cotton ball in alcohol, preparing himself for its sting. Any bad feelings floating around his head were cleansed away with the pain of the alcohol.

Frankie slid on a fresh pair of pajama bottoms and placed his towels in the bathroom hamper. He slipped back into bed and willed himself to go back to sleep. As his mind slid into the darkness, a shadow crept in. Frankie could hear Tanya calling for him once again. He tried to fight sleep and the dream he knew waited for him, but it was impossible. He was emotionally and physically exhausted. The chase began once again with the clinking of chains and darkness.

27

Jacob and Tanya talked as long as they could. Jacob felt he needed to protect Tanya. If Frankie was responsible for locking them in the shack, then, it was his fault Tanya was involved. He watched Tanya's head slide down the wall to his shoulder. She jerked back up. "Go ahead, Tanya, and lay your head on my shoulder. I've got you. Sleep if you can."

Tanya laid her head over on Jacob's shoulder. If only there was some way they could lie down. Jacob shook Tanya awake. "Let's try something here. Lie down on the front part of the cot. I'm going to try to lie down behind you. The chains will be a little uncomfortable, but I think we may be able to get some sleep this way."

Tanya lay down, and Jacob moved the chain, making sure it came over his legs. He didn't want her to feel pinned. The night air had a small chill to it, so he covered her with her jacket. He could feel the breeze slipping through the cracks in the shack. He slid down behind Tanya, sitting up only to adjust the chains. He pulled his jacket over himself, then listened to the bellow of a male alligator and something skittering outside the cabin. It was probably a raccoon trying to catch fish or some small critter. There were plenty of lizards around. They had skittered in and out of the cracks in the walls.

A sudden howl made Jacob stiffen. If he didn't know better, he would say he had heard a coyote. Tanya let out her breath. "Scared?" he asked her.

"I hate the sound of coyotes. They always sound so mournful and scary," she whispered.

"Wait," Jacob said, sitting halfway up. "You mean that really is a coyote? I thought they only lived out west?" He heard the howl again. This time, it was answered by several other howls and a tiny bark. Tanya began to giggle nervously. Jacob slid back down.

"Okay, what's so funny?" Jacob asked.

They heard the coyotes and the small dog again. Tanya giggled again. "I'd heard that a small dog was running with a pack of coyotes. I just didn't believe it. I figured they'd kill the dog. I guess I was wrong. That was definitely a dog barking along with the coyote's howling."

They listened for a while. The coyotes did not seem to be getting any closer. "Jacob?" Tanya turned until she was facing him. "Will you pray with me? I don't think I can sleep unless we pray."

Jacob slid his arm across Tanya. "Yes, I will. Close your eyes." He kissed her lightly on the forehead before he began. He prayed for their protection and for Frankie. He prayed God would send angels to protect them and look after their needs. He prayed that God would send someone to find them. Tanya relaxed in his arms. He continued to hold her until he could hear the soft purr of her breath. Only then did he close his eyes and slide into a dreamless sleep.

Jacob woke up to Tanya's back. She must have turned over during the night. He lay as still as possible so he wouldn't wake her. When she began to stir, he sat up, and as he did, he let out a gasp. Tanya sat up and looked at Jacob and saw him staring at something behind her. She was afraid to turn around but knew she had to. What she saw defied explanation. Sitting on the table was a pile of berries and six oranges. They both wondered if Frankie had returned in the middle of the night. As they sat up, they knew it hadn't been him. On the table were the muddy footprints of a raccoon. Jacob had prayed for God to supply their needs. He sent fruit from one of his own creatures. It was probably the raccoon Jacob had heard the night before.

Tanya and Jacob repeated the bathroom ritual they had performed the morning before. She pulled hand sanitizer from her backpack and passed it to Jacob. Tanya peeled an orange, separating it into its individual slices. She bit into one and cooed. This was the sweetest and juiciest orange she had ever eaten. She finished it off and pulled the water from the cooler. Pouring a small amount into her cup, she sipped it slowly. She looked over at Jacob. The juice from the orange ran down his chin. He had the biggest smile on his face.

After eating, they sat back on the cot. Jacob didn't know what to do. There was only so much you could do when you were locked up with nothing to do. "I've got it. Tanya, if we keep sitting on this cot, we're just going to get stiffer. We haven't really seen how far we can get in the cabin with these chains on." He stood up and walked until the chain was tight against his leg. He found himself a little past halfway across the cabin. There was no way he could reach a window or door. The only window they had access to was the one behind them. There was no screen in it. They had contemplated busting it out. The problem with that was there was no way to keep the animals out, and no way to shut it tight again. Tanya found that she could walk about three steps further than Jacob. They paced back-and-forth to keep the blood flowing in their lower legs. After about ten minutes, they sat down. Tanya reached for her purse. She remembered she had a book and a notebook in it.

"So Jacob, would you like to read or write?"

Jacob laughed. "I think I'll borrow a pencil if you have one."

Tanya reached into her purse and pulled out one of many pencils and handed it to Jacob. She watched him as he began to write on top of the table. He seemed so secretive. "Jacob, what are you writing?"

He looked at her and smiled. "I'm writing song lyrics."

"I didn't know you wrote songs," Tanya said. Jacob just smiled at her and continued writing. They passed the day writing or reading, pacing back-and-forth for exercise, and eating an orange for lunch.

Before they lay down to sleep, they knelt in front of the cot and prayed. They prayed that someone would find them soon.

CHAPTER

28

Frankie woke up more exhausted than when he had gone to bed. His body was sore as if he had been running a marathon. From the looks of his sheets, he had run the marathon on his bed. He walked to the bathroom to take a shower, glancing at the mirror as he passed it. He didn't recognize the face that looked back at him. The circles under his eyes resembled a lunar eclipse. He looked older but not in a good way. He remembered that presidents aged faster when faced with some sort of chaotic stressor. He could put himself in the same category.

He stepped into the shower, hoping to wash away the heavy feeling. He stood, letting the water stream over him until it ran cold. He stepped out of the shower and toweled off. The heaviness he felt had not left him. He tried to put on a happy face as he left his room. He didn't need his parents worrying about him. They already had too much on their mind.

Frankie's mom gasped when he entered the kitchen. His dad turned to look at him.

"Good morning," he said to his mom and dad.

Mr. Bonita looked at his son. It was apparent he hadn't slept well. "I guess I don't need to ask if you slept okay."

Frankie shook his head. "I feel like I was in a Charles Dickens book. I kept hearing chains rattling and Tanya and Jacob calling my name. I kept running, but all I saw was shadows and darkness. I feel a heaviness I've never felt before."

"Did you pray before you went to bed, son?" Mr. Bonita asked.

Frankie hung his head. "I guess I didn't, Dad. That probably would have helped. How did you and Mom make out last night?"

Frankie's mom stood up and walked to him, giving him a hug. "We slept peacefully. I was so upset when I went to bed. I figured I wouldn't be able to sleep. I heard your dad get up, so I rolled over and began to pray for him. I fell asleep feeling at peace about everything."

Frankie looked at his dad. "What about you, Dad? How did you sleep?"

"Well, Frankie, like your mother said, I got up and came into the living room. I prayed for quite a while. I felt like I needed to get up and go to bed, and when my head hit the pillow, I felt completely at peace. It was as if I had an angel breathing peace over us in the room."

Frankie looked frustrated. He needed that peace. It wasn't fair that everyone around him had it but him. He drank a glass of orange juice, then rinsed the glass and left it in the sink. He took one more look at his parents and went back to his room. He dressed in jeans and T-shirt and put on a good pair of sneakers. He wanted to be ready to join the search for his sister. He joined his mom and dad in the living room. They knelt and prayed before they left to meet the sheriff.

The volunteers met in Jasper Park. This was pretty central to everything. Sheriff Joseph was standing beside his police cruiser with a map on the hood. It looked like a scene right out of a movie. Volunteers stood around in groups. Jacob's parents were standing next to the sheriff when they saw the Bonita family and walked toward them. They exchanged hugs. Mrs. Wingate held onto Frankie longer than usual, seeing the pain in his eyes. She knew he hadn't slept well. She had spent a large part of the night praying for him. She didn't know why, just that she needed to pray for him. She had known for quite some time that something was bothering him. God had laid it on her heart to pray for him daily. As she hugged him, she prayed over him. His body seemed to relax a little. He smiled down at her and gave her a kiss on the cheek. "Thank you," he said before he walked away.

The sheriff divided the volunteers into groups. The last they knew Jacob and Tanya were headed to the movies. The sheriff sent a group of volunteers to check all the back roads going to the mall. They were going door to door to see if anyone had any information or had seen anything. Dive teams were in each of the waterways looking for any sign of Jacob's car. If it had left the road, it would be found.

Jacob, his parents, and the Wingates were asked to stay with the sheriff. Frankie protested. The sheriff pulled him aside. "Frankie," he said, laying his hand on Frankie's shoulder, "I know you want to be out there with the others. I need someone here just in case the news is not good. I need someone who can be strong. I know this is your sister and your best friend. However, these are their children. If the news is bad, I need to rely on you. It's never an easy task to bring bad news to the family. It's easier if there is someone with them." Frankie nodded agreement. He would do as the sheriff asked.

The sheriff knew the family wanted to get out and help. He'd been on many searches like this. The last thing he needed was the parents or brother to stumble across the bodies. That had happened only once in his career, and he vowed never to let the family join the search. The families waited with him, providing valuable information about their children.

It was shortly after lunch that the sheriff noticed a change in the preacher. Betsy, his wife, noticed it as well. Mr. Wingate sat at a picnic table in the park with his head in his hands. Betsy approached and saw his shoulders shaking. She sat across from him. He lifted his tear-stained eyes and looked at his wife. "This is all my fault, Betsy."

Betsy looked worried. "What do you mean this is all your fault. How could this be your fault?"

Her husband looked up at her. "God is punishing us for my sins. You know the scripture about the sins of the father being visited upon his son."

"Jacob, I do know the scripture, and I know that they are referring to the effects of a father's sin. It doesn't mean if the father sins, then, their sons will be punished. You had preached on this right before we left Illinois."

"No, Betsy, you don't understand. When I was in seminary before I met you, I had a girl I was engaged to."

"You're talking about Selma. I know her death was hard on you."

Daniel grabbed his wife's hands. "Please, Betsy, just shut up and listen to me. She died because of me. In a moment of weakness, I slept with her, and she got pregnant. I was afraid of what would happen to me. I mean, I was in seminary to be a preacher. What kind of preacher gets a girl pregnant when they aren't married? Then, I made things worse. I convinced her to get an abortion. It goes completely against everything you and I believe in. Selma agreed with me. She was fine after the abortion. I should say she was physically fine. The idea that she had killed our unborn child was too much for her. She became depressed, and they put her on medication for the depression. She was driving home when she fell asleep at the wheel and ran off the road. She died instantly. If I had not forced her to have the abortion, she would not have been depressed and been on those pills. I made her kill our child, and God is finally punishing me for it. I've tried to make everyone think I am so holy because I've never felt clean and forgiven for that act. That's why I know God is punishing us."

Betsy stood up and went to the other side of the table. She held her husband as he sobbed. Mr. and Mrs. Bonita looked over and rushed to the Wingates, assuming the worst. Betsy shook her head. Daniel looked up at the Bonitas. "Please, pray with me. No, pray for me. I am a sinner. I can't bear this alone." The four of them held hands and knelt on the ground. They prayed and cried out to God to ease their pain.

Sheriff Joseph had seen families strengthened by prayer. He bowed his head and said his own prayer for the family. When he looked up, he saw an agitated look on Frankie's face. Frankie walked away. Everyone was praying except him. Every time he tried to pray, he hit a brick wall. Why had God blocked him? Wasn't he good enough to have God listen to him anymore?

As the sun set on another day, the volunteers returned, dejected. They had wanted to find these teens. It had been three days since the parents had last seen them, and they knew the chances of finding them was getting slimmer. Even finding them dead would give the parents closure. There was nothing worse than never knowing what had happened to your loved one. They loaded up and went home, vowing to hug their own children a little tighter that night.

The sheriff assured the Wingates and Bonitas that they would begin again in the morning. He waited until they had left before he and his deputies drove off. He prayed that tomorrow would be the day he could return their children to them.

29

Tanya woke first and slid off of the cot. She needed some water and the bathroom. Reaching for her cup, she spilled the remaining contents on the table. She began to cry.

Jacob stirred. "Hey, Tanya, why the tears?"

She looked at him. "I spilled my water." Jacob laughed, and this brought on a fresh batch of tears.

"Hey, I was laughing because I had heard of crying over spilled milk but never over water."

Tanya's crying became hiccups as she began to laugh and cry at the same time. Jacob grabbed her and hugged her. "It's going to be okay. Let's take care of the bathroom issue, and then, we'll go from there." In the beginning, the bathroom situation was embarrassing. Tanya no longer cared. When nature called, you had no choice. She started to giggle.

"All right, Tanya, what's so funny now?" Jacob asked.

She tried to stop giggling. "I was thinking about how embarrassed I was the first time we had to do this and how now I could care less. Then, my mind wandered back to Bible times. I started to wonder what they did when they were out in the desert, and there was a whole bunch of tents around families everywhere. How embarrassing would that be? What did they say? 'Oh, hey, I'm going to go behind that dune over there, so if you would please stay here, I'd appreciate it.' Can't you just picture that?" By now Tanya was laughing hysterically. Jacob made her sit on the cot. Every now and then, he could hear a giggle behind his back.

Jacob looked at the food they had left—two donuts, one orange, and half a bag of chips. There was about a cup of soda left. There was a full cup of water left from the melted ice. Warm water was better than no water. Jacob thought about it. If they ate the chips, they would be extremely thirsty. The same thing would happen with the donuts because of the sugar. They needed the sugar from the orange and donut. Jacob decided they would split one of the donuts for their breakfast. He reached for the donut and found it covered with ants. They had made their way up the table and were all over the donuts. Jacob tried to get them off of the donuts without success. He tossed the ant-covered donuts across the room. He grabbed the bag of chips and found more bugs. He crushed the bag of chips into a ball and tossed it across the room with the donuts. Tanya looked at him. Jacob smiled at her. "We still have the orange."

Tanya burst into tears as she picked up the orange. The bottom of the orange was rotted out. "Why, Jacob? Why would God give us food and, then, let it be rotted or taken over by bugs?"

Jacob hugged her tight. "I don't know, Tanya, but I'm sure God had a reason. Let's just sit and conserve our energy." Jacob picked up the bottle of soda and examined it. He unscrewed the lid and took a sip, enough to wet his throat. He passed the bottle to Tanya, and she did the same. They spent most of the morning sitting or lying on the cot.

"It must be very humid outside," Jacob said. "I'm sweating so much. I just want some fresh air." He reached for the bottle of soda. It was empty. He poured the last of the water into the cup and handed it to Tanya. "That's all we have left. I hope your brother comes back soon." Tanya drank half and gave the rest to Jacob. His throat felt like it was lined with sandpaper. He tipped the cup up and drained it dry. They sat on the cot, leaning against the wall, praying for any type of breeze to squeeze through the cracks. Jacob got up from the bed and lay on the floor. "Tanya, come down here, the floor is cool. I can feel a slight breeze coming through the floorboards."

Tanya lowered herself from the cot to the floor. She stretched out like Jacob. If she was very still, she could feel the breeze. It wasn't much, but it was better than nothing. As the temperature rose in the shack, Jacob and Tanya felt more lethargic. Covered with sweat, Tanya could feel herself drifting off. She wondered if she would ever wake up. She saw one lonely sunbeam slipping through the French doors. In all the time they had been in the shack, the sun had never reached inside. She smiled, thinking of the cartoon with the little girl, Trixie, who sat in the sunbeam and talked to it. Like Trixie, Tanya reached for the sunbeam before she fell asleep.

* * * * *

Marcus Wilson had not been on the river for years. He had worked hard all of his life. He raised his kids after his wife passed away, never getting remarried. His kids were grown and had kids of their own. He had celebrated fifty years at the same plant. After retiring the week before, Marcus decided to take a vacation. He had rented a cabin at a nearby campground and decided he would like to get back out on the water. He rented a canoe, took a map, and headed up the river.

Marcus had always loved nature. He knew quite a bit from growing up in the swamps. His parents didn't have a lot of money when he was growing up, but they never went hungry. The swamp and the good Lord always provided food for them. Marcus had paddled for about two hours. He'd brought along a small lunch and a cooler of water. He knew he could go without food, but in this heat, he needed water. His phone rang. The display showed it was his daughter. He pulled up his paddles and drifted while he talked with her. He was telling her how much he was enjoying his relaxing vacation when he spotted the small shack. He put his daughter on speaker as he paddled toward the cabin. He paddled up to the land and stepped out of the canoe, pulling it up a little further onshore to make sure the current didn't grab it and take it back down the river.

Marcus reached down and grabbed his lunch and water as he stepped up on the porch. He described the shack to his daughter as he walked around it, telling her how the porch made a beautiful place to take a break and eat his lunch. As he came to the French doors, he glanced inside and gasped. "Tina, I gotta go. Two teens are lying on the floor inside, I think they're dead. They're chained to the wall. I gotta call the police. I'll talk to you later." He hung up the phone and dialed 911.

Marcus was new to the area. He told the sheriff where he was camping and described the direction he had paddled. He estimated he had paddled about six to eight miles. He asked if the sheriff wanted him to do anything more and was told to stay on the porch. They didn't want him going inside. He hung up the phone and called his daughter back. He explained to her about two teens who had gone missing. The sheriff thought they might be the ones. While he waited for the sheriff, he asked her to stay on the phone. They had talked and prayed together over the phone for the unknown teens inside the shack. He prayed help was not getting there too late. Marcus heard the sound of a boat engine. He told his daughter good-bye and hung up.

As the sheriff's boat came into sight. Marcus began to wave frantically. The sheriff pulled the boat up to the edge of the porch and handed a rope to Marcus. Marcus grabbed it and tied it to a post. He ran to the back of the boat and pulled it close and tied the rope to another post. He grabbed the sheriff's hand, helping him from the boat. The sheriff checked the glass door and found it locked. He stepped back and kicked the door in. The old wood crumbled, and the glass shattered. He ran across the floor, kneeling between them. He felt for a pulse, then called for two rescue units. He had found the teens alive but chained. They would need bolt cutters to get them free.

"Sheriff, is there anything I can do to help until someone gets here?" Marcus asked.

"Have you got any water left in that cooler? If you do, that would help, they look like they're very dehydrated. Marcus ran back to his canoe. He took out a towel he had brought with him. Using his knife, he cut a slit and, then, ripped the towel in half. He poured water on each piece and took them to the sheriff. They bathed their faces in the cold water.

Marcus and the sheriff could hear the sirens in the distance. The sheriff had not been near this cabin in years. As a boy, he had listened to the stories of it being haunted by the slaves who had died in it. He looked at the chains attached to the teens and noticed Marcus looking at the same thing. "What kind of person would chain kids up? Why would they even have a shack with chains?" Marcus asked. The sheriff explained the history of the cabin.

When the paramedics arrived, they took over. They came with backboards. They figured it would be easier to carry them out on them than trying to get the gurney down the bumpy wooded path to the cabin.

They quickly cut the locks from the manacles and strapped the teens to the backboards and carried them through the woods. After setting the backboards down, they pulled the gurneys from the back of the rescue vehicle. They placed each backboard on a stretcher, strapping it down. Once they had the gurney loaded, they began working with the teens. They started IVs to help with the dehydration. Once the IV was in, the driver closed up the back of the vehicle and headed for the hospital. He left the other paramedic in the back with the patients to handle all of the vital information.

The sheriff and Marcus headed back to the cabin. "Marcus, put that canoe in the boat, and I'll take you back with me to the campground. I'll need you to come in to get more information from you, if that's okay with you."

Marcus did as the sheriff asked. He untied the boat and stepped in. What had taken him a couple of hours of travel time took only fifteen minutes to get back to the campground. The owner of the campground helped the sheriff and Marcus out of the boat. Marcus unloaded the canoe. "Leave it with the owner, Marcus. You can settle up with him when I bring you back. We need to get to the hospital."

Marcus ran to catch up with the sheriff. No sooner had he fastened his seatbelt than they took off, sirens blaring. The sheriff called his office. "I need you to send cars out to the Wingate and Bonita homes and bring them to the hospital. Tell them we found their children alive, and they are headed to Sarasota Memorial Hospital."

30

In the middle of English class, Frankie was called to the office. He was told to come with all of his things. The class giggled as he got up. He wondered what they were going to accuse him of this time. He had just been admitted back to school. Didn't they know it was hard enough coming back after all he had been through?

To make matters worse, his parents had forced him to go to school today, knowing his sister was still missing. That seemed to be the only thing anyone wanted to talk about. He didn't have any answers for them. It was just a painful reminder that he was here and his sister was somewhere out there in the world, going through who knew what. As he walked into the office, he saw smiles plastered on the faces of those in the office. It was almost creepy.

The lady at the front desk could not contain herself. "They found Tanya and Jacob," she blurted out. "They're at Sarasota Memorial Hospital. I've already signed you out. Go, get out of here." Frankie ran to his car and threw his backpack into the back seat. He saw the officer sitting in his car and decided to leave the parking lot at the posted speed. Once on the street, he stepped on the gas and sped toward the hospital. He parked in the parking garage and ran inside to the information desk.

"Can you please tell me what room Tanya Bonita is in?" The lady behind the desk gave him the room number and directions to get there. Frankie's sneakers echoed in the hallway as he ran to the elevator. His heart was pounding as he stepped onto the elevator. He could hear the swooshing of blood flowing in his head. The elevator seemed to crawl. After what seemed like forever, he was able to step off the elevator and head to his sister's room. As he entered, he saw his sister and Jacob in separate beds. This was unusual. *They usually separated patients by gender*, he thought. However, since he had never been in the hospital, he didn't really know. They were both sitting up, eating. He noticed an IV delivering much-needed fluids. He looked around the room and wondered where his parents were. Had they even made it here yet? He rushed to Tanya's bed, knocking her food tray out of the way as he hugged her. Tears ran down their faces. He stepped away from Tanya's bed and stepped over to Jacob, grabbing his arm and pumping it.

"Man, I've been worried sick since the day I found out you two were missing. What happened, man, where were you guys?"

Jacob looked perplexed. He was sure it was Frankie who was responsible for locking them in that shack. Was he faking it to keep himself out of trouble? He just stared at Frankie with eyes wide open.

Frankie stared back at Jacob. "What? Why are you looking at me that way? You're scaring me?"

Jacob looked over at Tanya. "Frankie, didn't you lock us there?"

The confused look on Frankie's face convinced Jacob that Frankie had no idea what he was talking about. "Frankie, how many people know about that old shack besides the three of us?"

Frankie pulled a chair up between their beds and watched his sister continue to eat. "I've only taken four or five guys out to the old shack, besides you and Tanya. What does that have to do with where you guys were?" Frankie asked.

Tanya answered before Jacob had a chance. "Frankie, we've been locked in that shack ever since the night we met you there."

"What do you mean you've been locked in that shack? Who took you there? Why would they take you there? Did they hurt you?"

It was Tanya's turn to look confused. She was sure she could get the truth out of Frankie.

"Those are excellent questions, young man," Sheriff Joseph said to Frankie. "We've been wondering those very things."

Frankie noticed a man standing behind the sheriff. He pointed to him. "Who is he?"

The sheriff grabbed Marcus by the shoulder and led him into the room. "This is the gentleman you can thank for finding Tanya and Jacob. If he hadn't been on that river and decided that shack looked like a nice place to eat lunch, then, they might not have been found for quite a while. People seldom paddle that direction when leaving the camping grounds. They usually head toward Blue Springs, the other direction."

Frankie looked suspiciously at Marcus and asked, "Just why did you head the opposite direction?"

Marcus looked at Frankie square in the eyes. "I've just recently retired. I'm here on vacation. Everyone heading out that morning was heading toward Blue Springs. I wanted to relax and enjoy nature. I headed to the right. I figured I'd paddle for a couple of hours and watch the animals and just enjoy nature. When I was hungry, I'd just pull in the paddles and drift while I ate my lunch. Then, I saw the cabin. I was on the phone with my daughter and told her about the cabin with a porch, and I figured I'd stop and eat lunch there. That's when I looked in those glass doors and saw these two," he said as he pointed at Jacob and Tanya.

Frankie's attitude changed. He stood up and walked to Marcus, holding out his hand. "I'd like to thank you for finding my sister and best friend." He was surprised when Marcus took his hand and pulled him into a hug.

"I'm glad God put me in the right place at the right time, son." He released Frankie and looked him in the eye.

The sheriff clapped Marcus on the back. "What do you say I take you back to the campground so you can get on with your vacation?"

"Sounds great to me," Marcus replied.

Frankie sat back down in the chair as the sheriff and Marcus walked out of the room. "That was strange. Do you think he is on the up and up? Do you recognize him? Could he have been the one to lock you in there and, then, pretend to find you?" Frankie asked Tanya and Jacob.

Jacob looked first at Tanya and, then, at Frankie. "No, I don't think so. If it wasn't you, Frankie, then, I don't know what happened. That scares me more than thinking you might have had something to do with it."

"Jacob Wingate, how dare you accuse Frankie of kidnapping you and Tanya and locking you in that horrible place?" Mrs. Bonita scolded as she entered the room. "Why in the world would you even think something like that? Tanya, surely, you don't think your brother had anything to do with this, do you?"

Tanya didn't want to hurt her mom or her brother. "Well, Jacob and I came to that conclusion because we couldn't figure any other way we ended up in that shack."

Mr. Bonita had entered the room with the Wingates. "What do you mean you couldn't figure any other way? Have you been to that shack before?"

Frankie spoke up quickly, "Yes, Dad. When we used to have fights, and I would leave the house, that's where I'd go. I went walking through the woods one day and found it. It was all locked up. I cut the lock from the door and bought one to replace it. When I needed time away from you, that is where I went. I could sit and think and be totally away from everyone."

Frankie's dad looked down at the floor at the mention of the fights. He remembered his old self. It was tough to admit that life was so bad when he was drunk that it drove his own kid out of the house and made him feel he had to hide out somewhere. "Why didn't we know about this place?" He realized how stupid the question sounded as soon as it left his mouth.

"Dad, it was where I went to get away from you. It was also the place I would go and drink." Frankie stood and looked at his dad. "Yes, Dad, I would go there and drink. Not because I loved the taste of alcohol. I went there to numb my own mind from the pain of what was happening at home. I felt in control there."

Mr. Bonita grabbed his son and hugged him tightly. "Oh, son, I am so sorry for all those years I did that to you. I had no idea how much I had hurt the family. I always assumed that after I stopped drinking that you guys just forgave me and forgot. I guess I never wanted to look at that part of me and admit that I was the cause of all of the hurt and anger in our family. Can you ever forgive me?"

The easy thing would have been to tell his father that everything was all right and forgive him. Frankie decided he needed to be truthful. "I say this not to hurt you but because you need to hear it. I love you very much, Dad. I would die for you if I had to. But as far as being able to forgive you for the past? I've been working on that one for a long time. I won't lie and say I can or will. I can only tell you that I can work on it."

Mr. Bonita stepped back as if he had been slapped. He understood the painful words his son had spoken. "Fair enough, Frankie. All I ask is that you try."

Pastor Wingate stepped up to Frankie and his father. "This is a step in the right direction for both of you. Frankie, just remember what the Bible says about forgiveness."

Before he could say any more, Jacob interrupted. "Dad," he said with a severe tone in his voice, "not now." He stared his father down. He hated how his dad always had to interject the Bible into every situation. There were times when it was better to pray instead of talk. Jacob was shocked to see his dad nod his head and back off. That had never happened before. Maybe they could work on their relationship.

Jacob noticed his mother standing by the door, watching everything. She had tears in her eyes as she watched the exchange between Jacob and his dad. She smiled proudly at Jacob and mouthed the words "thank you" before she stepped further into the room.

Mrs. Wingate put her arm through her husband's arm. "Has the doctor or anyone else been in?" Mr. Wingate shook his head. "Well, why don't we go sit in the waiting room until the doctor comes in? It is fairly crowded in here." She looked at her husband as she led him to the door. As they approached the nurses' desk, she asked to be notified when the doctor showed up, then she headed for the waiting room. She and her husband were the only two in the room.

"Betsy," her husband said as he sat in one of the chairs, "have I always come across as too preachy?"

Betsy wanted to approach this subject carefully. This was and had been a powder keg for years. "At times, you have prefaced everything you said with scripture. Sometimes I felt you were so legalistic when it came to the Bible that it was actually a turn off to people. It felt more like you were trying to preach someone into heaven, instead of loving them into heaven." She took her husband's hands and looked him in the eyes as she spoke. "I, sometimes, think you come across to someone like you are the only one who knows the Scripture and what is best for them. You come across as if you must tell them what the Bible says or constantly remind them what it says because they're too ignorant to know or understand it." Her husband lowered his head into his hands. Betsy continued to speak. "Sometimes you have to love someone, be there for them, and let God work in their life the way He sees fit, not the way *you* think God should work in their life."

Pastor Wingate looked at his wife. "Have I been that terrible all these years? Have I made people feel like less of a Christian?" He was afraid of what her answer would be but knew that he needed to hear it.

"Yes, Daniel," she said softly and gently. "There had been times when you treated people like you had all the answers, and only yours were the right ones. You did that not only to members of the congregation but also to Daniel and me. That's why they asked you to leave. The women of the church came to me and told me that their husbands were going to speak to you. If they could not resolve the issue, then, they were going to ask you to leave. They asked that I not interfere. They said they had been praying about it for some time, and they felt this was what God wanted them to do."

Pastor Wingate suddenly understood what Jacob had felt by not being told about the move and other decisions he had made on his son's behalf. He felt entirely blindsided by this information. It hurt. But he knew his wife was right. Betsy could see the pain she had caused her husband. She felt a burden lift from her shoulders that she had carried for such a long time.

The nurse stepped into the waiting room. "The doctor is on his way to the room, if you want to head that way."

Jacob and Tanya's parents listened to the doctor. Their kids had checked out okay. Besides being covered with mosquito bites and severely dehydrated, they seemed to be in excellent condition. He wanted to keep them overnight, just for observation. If they appeared to be okay the next day, he would release them in the afternoon. He suggested the parents leave and let them get some rest. They all needed rest. He walked with the parents and Frankie out into the hall and watched them head for the elevator. The doctor knew it was difficult for them to leave their children after they had just been found. He laid their charts on the nurses' desk and headed off to his next patient.

Jacob waited for Tanya to finish her meal before he said anything more to her. His stomach had turned sour after talking to Frankie. He noticed that Tanya was barely picking at her food. She laid her fork down and pushed her tray away.

"Jacob, do you think it's possible that Frankie didn't do this? I looked at his face, and I don't think he was lying to us. Is it possible that we were wrong? If Frankie had done this, surely, he would have come back and given us some food and water."

Jacob didn't answer right away. He understood what Tanya was talking about. From the look on Frankie's face, he was worried and didn't seem to know where they had been. But everything in his gut told him that Frankie was the reason they were in that shack. "I don't know, Tanya. We both thought he locked us there. But I agree with you. If Frankie is guilty of doing that to us, then, he is one terrific liar. I've never seen anyone that good. I just don't know what to think anymore. If it wasn't Frankie, then, who locked us there and why? What did they hope to gain?" Neither of them had an answer for that question.

"I think we're going to have to tell the sheriff everything that happened that night. That means that Frankie and I will be in trouble for the hit and run. But I think that's the only way we can find out what happened that night," Jacob told Tanya.

"Jacob, is it possible that someone heard Frankie or us talking about the accident and decided to blackmail Frankie by taking us?" Tanya asked.

Jacob rolled over in his bed and faced her. "At this point, we have more questions than answers, so I think anything is possible." He turned off his light, rolled over, and tried to sleep, leaving Tanya with her own confusing thoughts.

Mr. and Mrs. Wingate invited Frankie and his parents to lunch.

Frankie hugged Mrs. Wingate. "Thanks a lot, but I have home-work I need to get done. I'll grab a sandwich at home." He left them at the hospital parking lot and headed home.

The Wingates and Bonitas stopped at the closest Amish restau-rant. They just needed a home-cooked meal that they didn't have to cook. They also needed time to talk and process what had taken place. After placing their order, the conversation turned to how well their children looked.

Mrs. Wingate looked at Mrs. Bonita. "I can tell this has been really hard on Frankie. He doesn't look like he's slept since this all began. Are he and Tanya close?"

Mrs. Bonita smiled, thinking about how close her kids were. "When Jose and I had marital issues a few years back, our fights and arguments would get pretty loud." She reached over, taking hold of her husband's hand. His face was red with embarrassment. "Frankie would always comfort Tanya. He was her protector. I think that he feels responsible for not being there to protect her through whatever they went through."

Mrs. Wingate nodded as she sipped her coffee. She wished that when she and her husband had problems, Jacob would have had a sibling to cling to. He had been alone just as she had. She had seen the same look in Frankie's eyes that she had seen in Jacob's. Jacob often felt responsible for the arguments between his mom and dad. She knew he tried to step up to be the man and protect his mom. Both of them had been alone with their hurt and pain. There was no one from the church they could confide in. Everyone at church had been afraid to get close to them. They didn't want her husband's interference in their lives.

Mr. Wingate took a sip of his water and spoke up, "I guess we've all learned something from this ordeal. I've learned that I haven't set a good example for my church members or my family." He hung his head. "I've been pompous and overbearing. My attitude said, 'Do things the way I tell you the Bible says you should.' Betsy and I talked about that this afternoon. She pointed that out, and I know it is true. It's something I have to work on. I just ask for your forgiveness and for your prayers."

Mr. Bonita nodded his head. "You aren't the only one that needs to ask for forgiveness. About five years ago, I had a horrible drinking problem. I went to church with my family every Sunday. Unfortunately, I was in the bars most evenings, or sitting at home, drinking. I was an abusive drunk. I don't mean I beat my wife and kids up, although I'm ashamed to admit there was some physical violence. My words were my main weapon. I hurled them the way a gladiator would hurl a weapon, determined to do the most damage possible. Why my wife stayed with me all those years is something I may never understand. When I started to have problems with Frankie and the school, I thought maybe it was my fault. I didn't want to accept the blame for anything. I listened to what you said and took it to the next level. I went back to being that jerk that was verbally abusive. I took most of it out on Frankie. I guess through all my years of drinking, I saw Frankie not as a kid, but as a young man who had stepped into my role and was a better man than me. I guess I was jealous that I couldn't be that man."

Rosa Bonita looked at her husband. She was so proud of her husband for what he'd said. She knew that it took a lot of courage to admit those things, not only to her but also in front of their pastor. The conversation stopped as soon as the waitress sat the food on the table in front of them. The conversation resumed once the waitress had left.

Mrs. Bonita spoke as she cut her meat, not looking at her husband. "I stayed with you because I knew the man I married was still inside somewhere. I don't know what started your drinking, and I don't need to know. I'm just glad you found your way back to us. Now we need to be there for Frankie. He's been hurting for quite some time. I think he's in some kind of trouble and afraid to tell us. I'm worried if we push the issue, we'll push him over the edge and away from us." Mrs. Wingate nodded her head.

Mrs. Wingate nodded. "I sensed that the day we were out looking for the kids. God has been speaking to me to pray for Frankie. I don't know what the issue is, but I've been praying." The talk turned to other things as they ate their dinner. When the bill came to the table, there was a note in red marker. It merely said, "Paid in full," and was signed, "God's Servant." The waitress told them that she was asked not to identify who it was. The two families left the restaurant with a warm, peaceful feeling in their hearts.

When they returned home, Mrs. Wingate headed to the bedroom. It had been a long day. All she wanted to do was lie in bed and read until she was tired enough to sleep. She had picked up another Amish novel at the restaurant. They had been her favorite type of book for years. They were always humbling and inspirational.

Mr. Wingate headed into his office. He had to work on his sermon. This was going to be the hardest one to preach. In this sermon, he was going to come clean to his congregation. They needed to know why he had chosen them. They deserved to hear what kind of man he was. He needed to seek their forgiveness and ask them to pray for him. Everything was in God's hands now. He would either keep them there at this church he had come to love, or he would move them on to something else. Either way, he knew that God was dealing with him. Refining him the way an artisan refined gold. Hopefully, he would come through a better man.

CHAPTER
32

Frankie finished his homework, then packed his backpack. Frankie checked his closet and his drawers for his PE shirt. How could it be missing? He checked the laundry room. He would have to buy a new shirt. He set his alarm thirty minutes early so he would have time to go to the school store and buy another shirt. He changed into his pajamas and slid between the sheets. He was tired and so happy that Jacob and Tanya had been found safe and sound. It bothered him that someone was still out there. The someone who had locked his sister and friend in that shack. If he had stayed there alone that night, would he have been the victim? All of these thoughts ran through his mind as he slipped into sleep.

Sleep was not peaceful; the nightmare was back. Frankie was in the dark. He could no longer hear Tanya and Jacob crying out for him. Something or someone was in the night, chasing him. He saw the shack up ahead. He ran as fast as he could to it. He fumbled in his pockets for the key. He managed to get the lock off and slip inside, sliding the latch down just in time. Whatever had been chasing him outside the door was scratching to get in. He heard whispers but couldn't tell what they were saying. Whatever it was, it terrified him. His blood ran cold. He ran to the table, saw the pin, grabbed it, and stabbed himself. He waited for the euphoric feeling it usually brought. This time was different. It only brought pain. He stabbed himself fifty—a hundred times—and watched the blood pour down his leg. There was no relief, only torment. Why couldn't he find release?

Frankie sat up in bed, his pajamas soaked once again. He looked around in the darkness in a panic. Whatever had chased him in his dream had followed him from the nightmare into his room. He could feel his heart pounding out of his chest. He reached for his bedside lamp and turned it on, but it did not chase away the fear. He leaned back against the headboard and tried to pray. The words would not come to him. He stayed in that position until his body could handle the exhaustion no more, and he drifted off to sleep and back into the same nightmare.

Morning eventually came. Frankie woke up more exhausted than when he had gone to bed. He headed to the bathroom for a quick shower and, then, to breakfast. He sat at the table with a cup of coffee, watching his mom busy in the kitchen, fixing breakfast, and his dad reading the paper. Neither had looked up at him. Frankie's mother sat a plate of eggs and toast in front of him. He ate them without saying a word. As his mother sat down, she sent a worried glance to her husband's direction. He saw the look and put his paper down.

"Well, Frankie, did you get all of your homework done last night?" Frankie answered without looking up.

"Yeah, it was pretty easy. I had math and history. It only took me about an hour." He ate another forkful of food.

"Did you sleep well?" his mother asked, concerned.

"Not really. I'm still having the same nightmare I was having when Tanya and Jacob were missing. The only thing different is that I don't hear them calling for me to help them anymore. I feel like someone is chasing me through the darkness. I thought it would end since we found them, but it hasn't. I was thinking last night that if I had been out there alone, it could have been me locked in that shack," Frankie said.

Frankie's dad put his fork down. "Your mother and I were talking about that shack last night. We don't want you going back out there again. We don't know if there is someone evil out there in those woods. We're not going to risk your safety to find out. Is that clear?"

Frankie nodded. He understood the message.

He cleared his place at the table, rinsing the dishes before he put them in the sink. He grabbed his backpack, said goodbye, and headed out the door. He stopped, staring at his car. He could understand if he had one flat tire, but instead, he was looking at four. He looked around before running back to the house.

"Dad, someone slashed my tires. All four of them are flat." His dad ran outside. It was worse than Frankie had said. Along the driver's-side door was a deep gash. Someone had keyed Frankie's car. He went back inside and picked up the phone. "Frankie, put your bag down. You're not going to school today." When he reached the police, he asked to speak to Sheriff Joseph. He explained the situation and agreed to stay in the house until someone came out. He hung up the phone and called the school, letting them know the reason Frankie would not be there.

Frankie and his parents sat at the table, trying to figure out what was happening, when someone knocked at the door. Sheriff Joseph and a forensic team were outside. He asked Frankie and his dad to step outside. "That's the way I found it, Sheriff. I didn't touch it. When I saw all four tires were flat, I went back inside to get my dad."

Frankie's dad interjected, "I ran out when I saw how panicked Frankie was. That's when I noticed the scratch on the door and called you." The forensic team checked the area for evidence, took pictures, and dusted for fingerprints. Sheriff Joseph went back inside to talk with the family.

"Did any of you see or hear anything last night?"

"No, Sheriff, we had all been so exhausted after leaving the hospital. We came home and stayed here." The sheriff advised Frankie to go nowhere without a parent's knowledge and not to go out at night alone. Something was going on here, and he needed to find out soon before someone else got hurt or ended up dead.

33

Sheriff Joseph had stopped by the hospital after leaving the Bonitas. He wanted to check on the condition of the two teens. After getting the good news that they would be allowed to go home that afternoon, he headed back to work. His secretary, Janice, was sitting at her desk.

"Morning, Janice."

Janice continued typing without looking up. "Morning, Sheriff. I put your coffee on your desk when I saw you pull up. You have a meeting with the mayor at one o'clock today to go over your progress on the hit-and-run case. What kind of person hits an Amish person on a bicycle and, then, drives off and leaves them?" She turned and looked at the sheriff for an answer.

The sheriff looked at Janice and answered her with his question, "What kind of person chains two teens up in a cabin and leaves them to die?" He shook his head and turned toward his office. "Janice, call the Wingate and Bonita families and set an appointment for tomorrow morning around nine o'clock or ten o'clock. I need to meet with both families. Maybe I can get some clues from the kids before they forget those little details. That might help me catch the sick person who would do such a thing."

Janice heard the sheriff's door close a little harder than usual. She knew he was frustrated by this case. He took everything personally when it involved teens. He had been this way ever since he'd lost his son, the victim of a senseless robbery. Everyone in the office wondered if the sheriff would pull through. It had been tough on him.

Sheriff Joseph sat, looking over the notes he had taken. At first, he'd believed the brother was involved. It became apparent that Frankie was relieved the teens had been found. He could see the special bond between Frankie and his sister. It might be best if he talked with her before he spoke to her brother.

Now it seemed that Frankie was as much a target as the other two. Maybe he was the main target, and they just happened to get caught in the middle. The sheriff made a few notes before getting ready for his meeting with the mayor. He'd be glad when everything was back the way it was supposed to be in their small town.

At the hospital, Jacob was waking up. He hadn't slept well, tossing and turning. He'd been sure sure Frankie had left them there, but Frankie seemed shocked they'd been in the old shack all that time.

Jacob tried to remember everything that had happened that night. After arriving, they sat, talking and joking nervously with Frankie. They joked about the food they had brought. He remembered it was hard to keep his eyes open. The next thing he remembered was waking up next to Tanya. Jacob looked toward her bed, where she slept peacefully.

Jacob heard the breakfast cart coming down the hall, stopping and starting as they took breakfast into each patient's room. He heard Tanya stirring in the bed next to him, no doubt, awakened by the food cart. Tanya took one look at her breakfast and began to giggle.

Jacob looked over at her. "What is so funny? Only you could find something funny about your breakfast."

Tanya continued to laugh. "I was thinking about how I usually only eat a granola bar and drink a cup of coffee for breakfast. Then, I thought about how delicious those oranges and donuts looked like a banquet after a few days." Jacob knew when Tanya was emotional; her first reaction was to laugh. He tried to change the subject because the next emotion would bring out her tears. She'd cried enough over the last few days to last for months.

"I'm not sure I can eat these eggs," Jacob said. "I'm used to cooking my eggs in layers of butter. Of course, my eggs don't look like two yellow eyes staring up at me, begging me not to eat them." Jacob could hear Tanya choking and laughing at the same time. "I guess I'd better eat before you choke to death over there, after my entertaining performance this morning." He heard another snort come from Tanya's direction. They finished the rest of their breakfast without speaking to each other.

After breakfast, the nurse came in with towels. "You're free to take a shower whenever you wish this morning. I hear your parents are bringing in some fresh clothes. You may take your shower and put on one of those," she said, pointing to the gowns lying next to the towels. Tanya needed to take a shower. She asked the nurse to close the curtain between them. Tanya took the extra gown to use as a robe and walked to the bathroom with her towel. They had a small packet of shampoo and soap waiting for her. She showered as quickly as she could, then put on a clean gown. When she was back in her bed, she told Jacob he could take his shower if he wished. She could hear him as he padded past her curtain to the bathroom. He emerged a few minutes later. The nurse came in to take their vitals and pushed the curtain back. They spent the rest of the morning watching meaningless television shows or dozing off.

Lunch was pretty much like breakfast.

At two o'clock, they heard their parents coming down the hall to get them. The curtain was drawn between them so they could dress in the clothes their parents had brought, then waited for the wheelchairs that would take them to their cars. It felt good to be leaving the hospital and heading home. What they didn't know was that they were going to the police station.

34

Frankie was leaving the house when his phone rang. It was his father asking him to meet at the police station. They wanted a statement about what happened the evening Jacob and Tanya disappeared. Frankie hung up the phone and felt the darkness immediately return to him. He became agitated. It wasn't fair he had to give up his afternoons to sit in some cop's office while he listened to Jacob and Tanya tell the police they didn't know what had happened to them.

Tanya and Jacob rode with their own parents to the police station. Once inside, the parents were seated in a waiting area, and they were taken to two separate rooms. They watched Frankie come in and saw them lead him to a third room. Jacob couldn't see their parents anywhere. The sheriff came in and sat at the table across from Jacob.

"Okay, Jacob. I'm going to ask you some questions. One of my deputies is asking Tanya the same questions. When we are finished with you two, we'll talk with Frankie and see if he can shed any extra light on this situation. I'm going to be taping this to make sure we get all of the information. Okay?" Jacob nodded his head. "You'll need to answer aloud. The recorder can't pick up a head nod or shake."

Jacob blushed at his mistake. "Sure, I understand."

"Your parents said you were headed to the movies. Did you ever make it to the movies?" the sheriff asked.

"No, we weren't really headed to the movies. We were headed to the shack to talk to Frankie."

The sheriff looked up at Jacob. "Let me get this straight. You went to the shack. No one took you there?"

Jacob looked at the table, absently pulling at a hangnail on his finger. "No, sir, we weren't taken there. We went on our own free will."

"Okay, then, how did you end up chained to the wall?" the sheriff asked.

Jacob looked up. "That's just it, sir. I don't know. One minute, we are sitting there, eating donuts and drinking soda, and the next thing I know, I'm waking up next to Tanya, and we're chained to the wall."

Something was missing here. The sheriff knew he didn't have the whole story. "Okay, Jacob, I guess we need to back it up a little bit. Why were you and Tanya going to meet Frankie at the shack? Was it someplace you guys went to party?"

Jacob squirmed in his chair. "No, sir. We went to talk to Frankie about an accident."

The sheriff looked even more confused. "What accident would that be?"

Jacob looked at the sheriff, and the sheriff could see the fear in his eyes. "Sir, do I need to have a lawyer with me?"

The sheriff sat back in his chair. He definitely wasn't expecting that question. "Well, that depends, did you do something to break the law? If so, then, I would say you might need a lawyer." Jacob swallowed hard and squirmed some more. "Jacob, why don't you just tell me what happened, and if a law has been broken, then, I'll stop asking you questions and get your parents. They can decide whether you need a lawyer or not."

Jacob agreed and began his story. "A couple of weeks back, we—Frankie and me—were headed home. We had gone out to the shack for a while. He and his dad had been arguing. He was upset because he was being bullied by this teacher at school. His dad wasn't listening to him because the principal kept saying Frankie was causing the trouble. Anyway, we were on our way home, and it was foggy. As we came around a curve, a car's headlights blinded us. After the car had passed, there was suddenly a guy on a bicycle in front of us. Frankie clipped him." The sheriff watched Jacob twisting the ends of his T-shirt as he talked. "I watched him fall into the ditch. I don't know if he was hurt or dead. I begged Frankie to go back. He panicked and stepped on the gas. He told me I'd better not tell anyone. I was in the car, so I guess that makes me a criminal too."

Jacob sat back. He was still nervous, yet he felt as if a one-hundred-pound weight had been lifted off of his shoulders. He should have done this weeks ago. Then maybe none of this would have happened. The sheriff excused himself for a moment. When he returned, he had a case file in his hands.

"We've had an unsolved case for the last couple of weeks. An Amish man by the name of Isaac Zook was found lying in a ditch on Chauncey drive. He was slightly injured. He ended up with a broken arm. He was fortunate he wasn't killed. Unfortunately, his bicycle was not so lucky. It was completely destroyed. Since you weren't a suspect at the time, and no one had asked you anything about it, and you hadn't lied to us, you are in the clear. However, even though you are in the clear, legally, you were morally wrong. You should have told someone. Why didn't you?"

Jacob looked up at the sheriff. "You didn't see the look in Frankie's eyes that night. I was more scared of him than what the law could do to me. He made it clear that I'd better not tell anyone or else."

The sheriff looked quizzically at Jacob. "Or else what?"

"I don't know what the or else was. The way he said it, I was sure if I told, he'd make sure I was sorry about it."

"You're sure you didn't tell anyone?"

Jacob shook his head. "The only one I told was Tanya. I know how wrong it was not to say anything. I couldn't tell my parents because they were in the Holy Land with church members. I couldn't tell Frankie's parents because I was staying with them. It got to the point where there was so much tension in the house, I couldn't eat or sleep. So a few days after my parents got home, I told Tanya. She agreed to help me convince Frankie that we needed to go to the police. I shouldn't have lied to my parents. I told them we were going to the movies. Instead, we met Frankie at the cabin."

The sheriff sat, listening. He was beginning to get a clearer picture of what might have happened. "Jacob, I'm going to talk with the deputy who's interviewing Tanya and compare your stories. Then, I'm going to do one of the hardest things I've had to do in a long time. I'm going out and talk with both of your parents and tell them about the accident. Then, I'll let your parents come in and talk with you. You do understand that just because there is no legal repercussion toward you, that you won't be off the hook with your parents. If they decide they want you to perform some sort of community service, I will back them."

Jacob nodded. He knew what was coming next was not going to be pretty.

35

The sheriff talked with the deputy who had interviewed Tanya. He found that her story backed up Jacob's. He learned that Frankie had been having trouble at home and school and that he had been cutting himself. He doubted Frankie's parents were aware of this problem. Kids usually did an excellent job of hiding it from their parents until it was almost too late. Typically, the kid got so depressed that he did something foolish like trying to kill himself. Often, they succeeded. He walked out to the waiting area to talk with the parents, knowing it would be challenging all the way around.

The sheriff sat down in front of both sets of parents. "Okay. We have some problems. It seems that your children have not been a-hundred-percent honest with you. Legally, Tanya and Jacob are in the clear. I haven't had a chance to talk with Frankie yet, so I don't know what is coming. However, I'm going to advise you to get a lawyer, Mr. Bonita. Do you have one?" Mr. and Mrs. Bonita looked shocked and shook their heads. The sheriff excused himself to make a call.

When the sheriff returned, he sat down, clasping his hands in front of him. He said a silent prayer for guidance. "It seems that while you," he pointed to the Wingates, "were in the Holy Land, you left your son in the care of the Bonitas." The preacher and his wife nodded their heads. "Well, during that time, Frankie was having some issues at school. He was very bothered by it, and according to both Jacob and Tanya, Frankie wasn't handling it well. According to Jacob, the problem was made worse by fighting at home over the situation." Both families nodded their heads. Up to this point, they already knew all of this information. "What you may not have known was that Frankie and Jacob had been out at the shack one evening when Frankie's day had gone south. According to Jacob, it was the only place Frankie felt he could talk it out and see his way through it. According to your daughter, Frankie has a history of cutting himself, and she's noticed cuts and scratches again. This tells me that your son is headed for a complete breakdown, if we don't get him some help. I'm just hoping it's not too late."

Frankie's father interrupted. "I don't quite follow you all the way. Why would that put my son in legal trouble?" He reached over and took his wife's hand for support.

The sheriff leaned back. "That's not what is putting your son in legal trouble. I'm trying to show you that there is a pattern of thinking here that leads up to what I am getting ready to tell you. On that particular night, as Jacob and Frankie were headed home in the fog, Frankie hit a bicyclist and left the scene of the accident. Jacob was in the car with him. Neither of them said anything to anyone."

The sheriff heard a door open and close. He turned and watched Kyle Black walk toward them. Kyle extended his hand to the sheriff. "Mr. and Mrs. Bonita, I would like you to meet Kyle Black, attorney at law. He's a public defender, since you have told me you don't have one and can't afford a lawyer. Kyle will represent Frankie when I go in to question him. He's going to go back to meet with him first. I've also asked our staff psychologist to sit in on the meeting to get his take on the situation. I want to do what is best for Frankie. I'm not here to put him away. We need to handle this very delicately. If not, Frankie could suffer a complete breakdown. Mr. and Mrs. Bonita, I'm going to take you back to see your daughter." He turned and looked at the Wingates. "I'll let you speak with Jacob." They all stood and walked to the interrogation rooms.

The sheriff left Jacob in the interrogation room to speak with his parents. A brochure fell out of the sheriff's notebook onto the table. Jacob picked it up and read it. One line stood out among them all. "How would you answer this question? Before I die I want to…" Jacob chuckled. It was a nervous laugh, not one of amusement. How would he answer that question? There are a lot of things he would want to do before he died. After all, he was a typical teen. But this question niggled at him. It required something more—maybe more than he was willing to admit. He sat back and began making a mental list of things he'd like to have or do before he died. He'd like to be able to change what happened that landed him in the sheriff's office. He'd like to become a great musician. All of these seemed like surface answers. No, he needed to answer this one from his soul. What is the one thing he wanted? The answer was there in his head. It had always been there. He had said these words to his dad and felt they were brushed aside. *Before I die, I want to know that my father truly loves and cares about me and not his image or his church.* This thought had been going through his head for so long, and he was afraid to voice it. He was fearful of the answer he might receive.

He put the brochure down when his parents came in. Jacob could tell the minute his dad walked through the door that he was in big-time trouble. He knew now was the time when he would find out the answer to that question.

Jacob's mother sat at the table across from her husband. She said nothing. Jacob looked at his dad. "Please, say something, Dad. I can't stand having you stare at me."

His father looked down at his hands. "I can't believe how much I've failed you, Jacob."

Jacob looked at his mom, then back at his dad. "What do you mean you failed me? This isn't your fault. It's mine and Frankie's."

His dad looked up at Jacob with pride. "I know you've willingly taken responsibility for your role in the accident. I've failed you because you didn't trust your mother or me enough to guide you down this path. You traveled it all alone. I can't imagine how you must have felt to be in that situation. You were loyal to your friend because you both loved him and feared him. It was a wrong choice, and one we need to figure out. We need to find a way to make amends to the man you wronged. Even though you were not behind the wheel, you were still partially responsible. You didn't even call paramedics to get help to him sooner. I don't know what we'll do about this situation, but we'll figure it out together, okay?"

Jacob looked from his dad to his mom. His mom was smiling at both of them. She spoke to Jacob as a young man, not as a child she had to protect. "Every mother wants to protect their children from the world, even if that world involves issues in the family. I've failed you by not allowing you to stand on your own two feet. Even when I knew you were wrong and your dad was right, I tried to make things better. I hindered your growth. I feel you grew to resent me for it. For that, I'm sorry to both of you. We can move on and grow strong together."

Jacob felt warm and safe. He knew the next few weeks were going to be rough. He leaned forward on the table. "What are they going to do to Frankie?"

Jacob's father rubbed his forehead. "They've brought in a lawyer to talk with him before the sheriff does. They're also asking a psychologist to sit in with the sheriff. Were you aware he was cutting himself? You haven't been cutting yourself, have you?"

Jacob had to laugh at that. "No, Dad, I haven't been cutting myself. I only found out about the cutting from Tanya. That's one of the reasons she was so concerned."

Jacob's dad reached over and patted his son's hand. "We're concerned too. As the pastor of his family, I think it should be a family effort for us to rally around them and support them. Most importantly, let's do this because they're our friends."

Mrs. Wingate looked at her husband. He had never allowed himself to get close to any of the congregation. Not close enough to call them friends. She felt like they had finally found a home in Strawberry Ridge.

* * * * *

The sheriff had gone in with the Bonitas to speak with Tanya. They were concerned about her. They wished she'd come to them when she first heard about the accident. She told them about her call to Frankie and how he'd agreed to turn himself in. She apologized to them for lying about the movies. She recounted all the funny things they'd talked about and about how she had felt dizzy, and Frankie had taken care of her. That was all she could tell them because all she remembered after that was waking up next to Jacob, locked inside the shack.

The sheriff had a theory about what had happened, and he'd have to see how it played through. He excused himself and headed to Frankie and his lawyer.

CHAPTER
36

The sheriff walked in with another man he didn't introduce. Officer Ortiz had been with the sheriff's department for over twenty-six years. He'd sat in on thousands of interrogations, taking notes, trying to figure out if there was an underlying issue. He sat back and prepared to write.

"Frankie, do you know why I asked for a lawyer to be present today?" the sheriff asked.

Frankie looked at his lawyer and, then, at the table. "Yes, sir, I do. It's because of the hit-and-run accident I was involved in. Did I kill the guy?" Frankie continued to look at the table.

The sheriff's tone was soft. "No, son, you didn't. We're trying to figure out what happened and why you didn't stop."

Frankie looked up toward the ceiling, as if he was trying to remember what had happened that night. "I was driving back from the shack. I go there, sometimes, when I am frustrated and sit and cool off. Sometimes I have a beer. I know I'm not of legal age, but I can always get it if I want it. Jacob and I went out there after Wednesday night church was over. I was still angry because of Mr. Fugate." Officer Ortiz took note of Frankie's tense body and clenched fists. "It wasn't fair that he was bullying me like he was, and no one would listen. The kids in the class were afraid to say anything because he threatened them. So they started taping his class and passing it on to my mom. My mom made my dad mad by going to see the principal. They argued about it a lot."

Frankie's jaw muscles tightened. He was speaking now with clenched teeth. "It wasn't fair that I had to act like nothing was wrong. And Jacob's dad came in and told my dad how to handle me like I was some little kid." Frankie slammed his fists on the table. His breathing became heavier. "So after church, we went to the shack. I ranted and raved to Jacob. He's been a great listener. On the way home, we came around a corner. It was foggy out, and I was temporarily blinded by the headlights of a car. I honestly didn't see the bicycle until it was too late. I swerved but still clipped him. I saw him fall over in the ditch. I knew I needed to stop. I panicked and kept going. There was no reason for me to do that, except I was scared to death. I accept responsibility for it."

The sheriff asked about the night that he, Tanya, and Jacob had gone to the shack.

"Jacob had told my sister about the hit-and-run accident. Did they tell you they're dating?" The sheriff just nodded. "Well, she called me and told me she knew about the hit-and-run. She pleaded with me to turn myself in. I was so tired of running. I told her to have Jacob bring her out to the shack the next night. I waited, and we had some snacks and talked about it. Jacob had fallen asleep at the table. I told Tanya I was going to turn myself in. I told her not to wake him until I'd been gone a while. I wanted to have my parents come with me. I know I went home. I don't know what happened after that. My head felt fuzzy. I woke up the next day to find you in my house and Jacob and Tanya missing."

The sheriff continued to write and not say anything. Officer Ortiz could feel the tension in the room and knew the sheriff was doing this on purpose. He glanced up at Frankie, who was frantically rubbing his hands back-and-forth on his jeans.

"Sheriff, am I going to be arrested?"

The sheriff looked up at Frankie. "I'm really sorry to have to tell you that you will be arrested. If bail can be made, you'll be released to your parent's custody." Frankie looked at his lawyer. The sheriff could see the fear in his eyes.

Mr. Black leaned over and patted Frankie on the arm. "Don't worry. By the time they have you processed, we'll have you bailed out. I'll come to your house tomorrow to tell you exactly how much trouble you're in." Frankie continued to rub his hands on his thighs, and Officer Ortiz continued observing and writing.

The sheriff stood Frankie up and led him out of the room to booking. As they came to the interrogation room where his sister and parents were, they stopped. They all hugged Frankie and told them they would be waiting for him. Jacob and his family had stepped into the hall as Frankie headed toward them. Once again, the sheriff stopped and allowed them to speak to Frankie.

"Are you mad at me for telling?" Jacob asked.

"No, man, I actually feel relieved. I wish I'd listened to you that first night."

Jacob's mom and dad stepped forward and hugged Frankie. "We'll be there supporting you all the way," Mr. Wingate said. Frankie nodded as they walked him down to booking. Tanya ran from her parent's side and buried her tear-filled eyes in Jacob's shirt. He held her tight, rocking her gently back-and-forth. They went back to the front to wait for Frankie's release.

CHAPTER 37

Officer Ortiz studied his notes as he waited for the sheriff. Obviously, Frankie had some problems. The least of these seemed to be the hit-and-run accident. He wished he could ask him more questions. His job was to sit and get a feel for the kid, not counsel him. However, he knew counseling was what Frankie needed. He read more of the transcript and jumped when he heard his door open. Sheriff Joseph plopped himself in the chair, massaging his forehead

"Okay, Ortiz, tell me what you think."

"Well, Sheriff, I think the kid has a lot of problems. Is he the one responsible for locking his sister and friend up?"

"I don't know yet. He seems to be blocking something. I'm just not sure what that is."

"There's definitely anger in him. His story is corroborated by his sister and Jacob. There has to be some clue left in the cabin that will tell us definitively whether he's responsible. I'll tell you right now that you're going to have to be careful when you talk to him. He's like a ticking time bomb."

"What do you mean a ticking time bomb? Are you saying he could get violent?"

"No, Sheriff, what I'm saying is that he looks like he could go over the edge at any moment and have a complete breakdown. He could be pushed to the point of ending up in a mental facility.

If that happens, then I can guarantee we may never find out what happened."

The sheriff looked at Ortiz and began massaging his head again. His headache seemed to be getting worse, the longer he thought about this case. Strawberry Ridge was a small town, and he didn't usually see such excitement. He really wished that things could go back to the way it had been—just a peaceful, quiet town.

Officer Ortiz looked over the transcript again and made a list of things he needed to do. First on his list was a trip to the school. He needed to talk with some of the students to find out what had been happening with this teacher. Maybe they had seen some signs that no one else had seen. He also needed to talk to Jacob and Tanya to see what they might be hiding.

38

Officer Ortiz walked into the sheriff's office, notepad on one hand and a cup of coffee on the other. He lowered himself quietly into a chair in front of the desk and waited for the sheriff to finish his phone call. As soon as the call was finished, Sheriff Joseph leaned forward.

"Okay, Ortiz, what did you find out?" He rubbed his temples before looking up. It wasn't even noon yet, and he knew it was going to be a long day.

"Well, Sheriff, I talked to, at least, a half-dozen kids in Frankie's class. They all said pretty much the same thing. Frankie started falling apart about three weeks ago. They said Mr. Fugate had started picking on Frankie, but no one ever said anything. Then, three weeks ago, Frankie pulled into the school parking lot. Mr. Fugate saw him and noticed a small dent in the front fender of his car. According to the kids, the teacher asked Frankie if someone had finally come to their senses and tried to take him out? When Frankie asked what he meant, he was told by Mr. Fugate that he just thought it was about time someone tried to run a greaser like him out of the country or off of the road. Either was fine by him. They said that's when they noticed the change in Frankie.

"Mr. Fugate seemed to get under Frankie's skin, and he knew it. He took every available opportunity to torture Frankie, mentally and verbally. When he started lying about Frankie and got him suspended and, then, threatened the class with failing grades if they opened their mouths, they decided it was time to take action. That's when they started taping his class. The more the principal believed Mr. Fugate, the more trouble Frankie got into at home. He was in a no-win situation. He was caught in the middle with no one to believe him except his mom. Frankie felt she was powerless to help. If he had something to do with Tanya and Jacob's being held in the shack, then, it was probably a reaction brought on by the pressure from Tanya and Jacob to turn himself in for the hit-and-run. He probably felt the last people on his side had just turned against him. If that is the case, then, I would say he just snapped. Coupled with the lack of sleep, you have all of the ingredients for a breakdown."

"Okay, I get all that. But how could Frankie not remember he did this to his own sister? Good grief, it seems like he would realize what he'd done, and that would be that."

Ortiz sighed. "Remember, Sheriff, I said *if*. What we do next must be carefully planned."

Sheriff Joseph stood and walked around the desk, perching on the edge of it. "What do you propose we do?"

Ortiz began to gather up all of his things and stood. "What I suggest is that we go over that shack with a fine-tooth comb. Once we're sure we've collected everything we can, we take the kids back there. Maybe it will trigger some memories. I guess we'll have to keep our fingers crossed and hope for the best."

The sheriff nodded and stood up. He held out his hand; Ortiz grabbed it and pumped it up and down. "Thanks for looking into this for me. I'll let you know in just a little while how we're going to proceed."

Ortiz walked to the door and grabbed the doorknob. He turned and looked back at the sheriff. "Just remember what I said. It won't take much to push him over the edge, so be very careful." He walked out of the office, closing the door behind him.

The sheriff knew he needed a break in this case. He just didn't want that break to be Frankie's mind. He took out a pad and pen and began to write a list. First, take a deputy back to the shack to go over every inch, inside and out. He listed the things he wanted to zoom in on when he took the kids back to the woods. He needed to know what time they got to the shack, then walk them through, step-by-step, in hopes something would break in the case.

Sheriff Joseph grabbed his jacket and left his office. He grabbed Deputy Turner on his way out. When they arrived at the shack, they first inspected the doors and windows. There were a couple of animal prints but nothing else. Next, they went inside and noted where everything was. One of the reasons he had selected Deputy Tuner was because he had an eye for detail. He could tell that nothing would be missed. Deputy Turner was the first one to spot the T-shirt. It was wedged between the bed and the wall. He slid on a pair of gloves and carefully pulled it out. They looked it over before putting it in an evidence bag. The cooler where Frankie kept the drinks was still there. There was a small pool of stagnant water inside. They collected every loose item they could find in the cabin and dusted for fingerprints.

Sheriff Joseph found a small bucket under the bed and pulled it out. He realized what it was and shoved it back, but not before the smell had floated up to his nostrils. The sheriff gagged as he took the bucket outside and dumped it near a tree. That's when he saw the bottle lying on the ground. He picked it up and read the label before putting it in an evidence bag. When there was nothing else to photograph, they packed up their gear and went back to the station.

Sheriff Joseph walked into the lab at the police station. "I do hope you can find someone who can process this for me." He handed the lab tech everything they had collected.

Kyle Black sat at the kitchen table in the Bonita home. Frankie sipped his coffee nervously, watching Mr. Black pull out his notepad and several official-looking pieces of paper. He glanced at his parents. He was ready to hear what type of punishment he would receive for the hit-and-run. No matter what happened, he felt at peace about it. It's funny how telling the truth made you feel so free.

"So Frankie, I spoke with Mr. Zook this morning. He's dropped all charges against you. The state could go ahead and prosecute. However, it's against Mr. Zook's religious beliefs to take you to a court or testify against you, so I'm sure the state won't pursue it. This doesn't mean that you're off the hook. Mr. Zook owns a farm and has been unable to work for the last three weeks. We've come up with a solution to both of your problems. You will be working for Mr. Zook until such time as he can use his arm again. You'll work for no pay."

Frankie nodded his head as he blew out a breath. This could have been so much worse. It was a good thing he liked to work outdoors. "Since you're taking your classes online now, you'll start at eight o'clock in the morning and finish at four o'clock. He'll provide you with a lunch that you will eat with him. That part is absolutely nonnegotiable. Once his arm is working correctly, he'll pay you a small wage. Half of that wage will be kept to pay off the purchase of a new bike.

Frankie smiled with relief. "I can do all of that. However, I've already taken the money from my personal bank account and bought him a new bike. Sheriff Joseph showed me his old bike, and I bought him a new one—only better."

Mr. Black smiled. "Well, in that case, why don't you get dressed, load up the bike, and we'll drive over?" Frankie parked and removed the bicycle from the back of Mr. Black's truck and walked it to the porch. Mr. Zook stood from his chair and walked down the steps. Frankie, shoulder's drooped and head slightly bowed, walked to this man. What would he say to him? Mr. Zook held out his hand to Frankie and smiled.

"So you're the young man who is going to help me. Nice to meet you."

Frankie couldn't help but smile back. "Yes, sir, I am. But first I want to apologize to you for not stopping when I hit you. If I had it all to do over again, I would stop to help."

Mr. Zook looked at him, a gleam in his eyes. "If you had it all to do over again, I hope you wouldn't hit me." He stood, looking at Frankie, before he began to laugh. Frankie laughed with relief. This man had a sense of humor. He didn't know what he had expected.

"Mr. Zook, can I ask you a question? Why do you have a truck if you're Amish? I thought the Amish didn't drive motorized vehicles."

"You're right, Frankie, the Amish don't. I'm Amish-Mennonite. We have electricity and cars and phones. However, we aren't frivolous with our money." Frankie nodded his head. "Now, let's get our day started. I'll show you what needs to be done." Frankie followed Mr. Zook to his small barn. They grabbed some hoes and walked toward the field. "I've had this farm for several years. I came down from Ohio about twenty years ago with my wife. She helped me in the fields up until cancer took her last year. I have a small stand at the edge of my property where I sell what I grow. Some of my neighbors bring down their produce as well."

"What do you grow?" Frankie stepped up to the edge of the field. He'd never worked on a farm. "Wow, I see you have lettuce, cabbage, tomatoes."

"I have bell peppers, celery, cucumbers, and spinach, as well. We also have a grove with grapefruits, oranges, and tangerines. That field over there is my strawberry field. We produce some of the biggest strawberries in Strawberry Ridge."

"What would you like me to do out here?"

"Do you know how to use the hoe? If not, I'll show you, and you can start getting rid of some of those weeds. I'll show you the difference between the plants and weeds so you don't tear out the plant."

Frankie watched Mr. Zook quickly whack out the weeds with just one hand. He knew if Mr. Zook had to do this with one hand, the weeds would probably take over faster than he could get rid of them. Just the thought of helping keep all of those plants growing made Frankie feel proud. He worked steadily for a couple of hours. Mr. Zook came out with some water and walked him up to the house. It was lunchtime, and one of the church ladies had brought out some lunch for them. Frankie was curious as to why Mr. Zook required him to eat with him. They sat at the picnic table in the yard, and Mr. Zook blessed the food. "I heard you've had some trouble lately. I mean, besides hitting me. Tell me about it." Frankie swallowed hard. Why in the world would this man be interested in his problems? He told him about the trouble at school. He didn't know why, but he suddenly found himself telling him about the cutting.

"You do know that your body is God's temple, don't you?"

"Yes, sir, I do. I also know that what I've been doing is all wrong. I don't know why the pain relieves the stress, but it does."

"You're using the pain from cutting or poking or whatever you do to hide the pain you feel in here." He tapped Frankie in the chest. "This is where God is supposed to be, so why don't you let him handle the stress? I think he can do a much better job than you've been doing."

"May I ask you a question, Mr. Zook?"

"Only under the condition you call me Isaac and not Mr. Zook. I think we've worked together long enough today to consider each other friends."

Frankie smiled and nodded. "How were you able to just forgive me so easily after I did such a terrible thing. I mean, I left you in a ditch and drove off after I hit you. How could you just forgive me?"

"That's what God commands us to do. So if I didn't, I would be disobeying God." Frankie nodded and finished the rest of his lunch in silence. "Tell you what, Frankie. I'm pretty beat. What do you say we call it a day and start again tomorrow?"

"Great. I'll be here at eight o'clock in the morning. What would you like me to start on?"

"If you can finish the weeding in that field tomorrow, then maybe we can pick some of the vegetables. I need to open my produce stand."

"Sure thing, Mr. Zook—I mean, Isaac. I'll see you tomorrow."

Frankie drove home. Before he went inside, he called Jacob and left a message on his phone. "Dude, that guy is awesome. I was really nervous, but he's really nice. He had me weeding. Tomorrow, when I finish, we're bringing in some of the produce that's ready. He has a produce stand he runs. Gotta go, Jacob, got my homework to do." Frankie went into the house and straight to his room. His dad was surprised to find Frankie hard at work on his homework without being told. He was glad to see a change in his son. For the first time in a long time, Frankie seemed happy.

CHAPTER

40

Frankie left before his parents were up. The sun was just coming over the horizon. He wanted to make sure he got to the field early. As he backed down his drive, Frankie didn't see the car sitting down the road with his lights off. As soon as Frankie went around the first curve, the vehicle's lights came on and began to follow him. How could it be that he just kept having such good luck? Mr. Fugate watched Frankie turn into the farm. Why in the world would he be going there? Mr. Fugate read the name on the mailbox. He turned his car around and headed for Sarasota.

Mr. Fugate sat in front of the Amish market, waiting for it to open. Once inside, he walked around, gathering a few tomatoes and some peppers and approached the register. "These look really great. Do you guys grow them?"

"No, sir," the clerk replied. "We get them from local people like Jacob Yoder and Isaac Zook."

"Zook. Doesn't he have a place out in Strawberry Ridge? He has a little produce stand?"

"Yeah, that's him. He sells some out there and brings the extra in here."

"Did I read that someone hit him? Is he okay?" Mr. Fugate gathered up his bag and his change and waited for an answer.

"Yep, a teen hit him. He has him working for him now until his broken arm heals."

Mr. Fugate nodded thoughtfully. "Good, maybe it will work out for both of them. You have a great day." He walked to his car with all the information he needed. Now all he needed was to wait for the right time.

He drove past the farm, watching Frankie carrying vegetables to the barn. He watched him take fruits and vegetables to the stand. What Mr. Fugate needed was something that would cause Mr. Zook to lose faith in Frankie. He watched Frankie leave that evening, as a plan began to form in his mind.

Sunday morning, Mr. Fugate sat in his car, a quarter of a mile from Isaac Zook's house. He had to time everything right. He'd sat there since five that morning, waiting for Mr. Zook to leave his home. As Mr. Zook stepped into his truck, Mr. Fugate quickly stepped out of his car and opened his trunk. He removed his jack and sat it next to the tire. As Isaac approached his vehicle, he stood and picked up the jack and placed it into the trunk. Isaac would have no reason not to believe Mr. Fugate had just changed a tire. He closed the trunk and walked to the front of the car and slid into the seat. When he saw Isaac's taillights disappear, he started the car and turned into the drive. As he exited the car, he slipped on a pair of gloves. He didn't want to leave any fingerprints. He walked to the barn and grabbed a hoe. When he reached the row of spinach, he began chopping at the plants. He dropped the hoe and Frankie's hat next to it.

Frankie was so trusting that he hadn't thought he needed to lock his car at his own house. Mr. Fugate had walked up to Frankie's car and quietly opened the passenger door. All he took was Frankie's baseball cap. After leaving the hat and hoe in the field, he slid back into his car and left.

CHAPTER
41

Frankie pulled up to Isaac's house. Isaac sat on the porch with a hoe and a hat in his hands. "Hey, where'd you find my hat?" Frankie asked as he walked up to the porch. Isaac quietly handed the hat back to him.

"I found it in the field next to the hoe." Frankie looked at him, puzzled.

"What hoe? We put everything away yesterday when we finished."

Isaac looked up at Frankie. "Did I do something or say something to upset you yesterday?"

Frankie felt apprehensive. Why would Isaac ask him such a question? "Of course not, we've been good since day one. Why? What's happened?"

Isaac stood up. "Walk with me." They walked toward the field. Frankie could see the destruction before they reached it.

"Isaac, what happened?" He turned and saw Isaac staring at him. "You think I did this?"

"I did, Frankie, until I saw the look on your face. I came home from church yesterday and thought I'd grab a couple tomatoes for my lunch and saw this. I can't figure out why someone would want to do this. Well, let's get started. I want to finish the cucumbers today. We need to get some of those strawberries in as well."

"You got it." Frankie went to the cucumbers with a basket and knelt down. He remembered to look for cucumbers that were firm and about five to eight inches long. He took the clippers and started clipping the vines above them, working quickly. After his third trip to the barn, Isaac called him to lunch. He could tell something was still bothering Isaac. He sat down at the table and bowed his head. Isaac handed him a sandwich. "Frankie, something has been bothering me. How did your hat get out in the field? I remember you taking it off before you sat down in your car."

Frankie shook his head. "I have absolutely no idea. I've been wondering that myself." Frankie finished his lunch and waited in the strawberry field for Isaac to join him. Isaac explained the proper way to collect the strawberries. Frankie gathered the required amount and brought them up to the house. He helped Isaac load them into his truck. "Hop in. It's time you learn how to run the stand." Frankie did as he was told. He noticed a dark-green car parked down the road but thought nothing of it. They lived out in the country. People were always parking and taking in the scenery or calling someone to find directions.

He pulled the fruits and vegetables from the back of the truck and set it up under Isaac's guidance. It was almost as if everyone around knew when Isaac put fruits and vegetables out on his stand. They were suddenly swamped. Isaac talked with his friends while Frankie bagged the food and took the money. They had only worked two hours when he realized they were almost out of produce. Isaac threw his keys to Frankie and sent him back to the field for more. As Frankie unloaded the truck, a car pulled up, and his friends piled out.

"Hey, man, someone told me that you were working here. We miss you at school. How's it going anyway?" The questions came at him from all directions. Isaac watched with amusement. "Are you going to ask Amber to the prom?"

Frankie shook his head. "No, man, I need to just work and finish school and keep my head in the game. Besides, Mr. Grimhold said I'm not allowed back on school property until they solve the case with Mr. Fugate. I don't think that's fair. I'm still getting shafted here. It's not my fault he's prejudiced or that his wife ran off with someone else. He got what was coming to him, and I'm not sorry. I just want all of this to be over."

Isaac noticed the tension in Frankie's voice. He watched him clench his fists and his face turn red. This was an issue Frankie hadn't dealt with yet. He watched Frankie's buddies began to tease him and shove him around. They were trying to lighten the mood. The horseplay got rough. One of the boys grabbed a couple of oranges to play keep-away with Frankie. They bumped into the stand, knocking cucumbers and strawberries to the ground.

Isaac stood and, with a firm voice, said, "Frankie, I think it's time your friends left. This is not a playground. You're working here. Your friends will need to pay for any fruit or vegetables they damaged because they can't be sold."

Frankie looked down, embarrassed. "Sorry about that. You're right. Guys, you really need to leave. I'll see you around." He reached into his pocket and pulled out enough money to pay for the damaged food. His friends drove off, leaving Frankie with Isaac.

"Why did you pay for the food instead of making them pay for it?" Isaac asked.

"Because they were my friends, and I was just as responsible for the damage as they were."

"Frankie, you know you aren't responsible for everything that goes on, don't you?" Frankie dropped his head. "You still hold a lot of anger toward this Mr. Fugate, don't you?" Frankie looked up and began rubbing his hands on his thighs. Isaac saw this. "This is what makes you poke and cut yourself? Does this man hold that much power over you that you would allow him to continue to hurt you?" Isaac grabbed and hugged him while praying God would pour a vial of peace over Frankie.

Mr. Fugate sat and watched through a pair of binoculars. He'd seen the boys from school goofing off. Something they had said made Frankie mad. Whatever Frankie and Mr. Zook had talked about, Frankie was not in a good mood. He watched them close the shutters on the stand and Isaac place the money box into a particular slot and lock it up. Mr. Fugate watched Isaac slide the key into a slot at the top of the stand.

Frankie and Isaac drove back to the house. "I'm proud of you, Frankie, you've done a great job. You have no idea how big a help you've been. I'll see you back tomorrow morning. You know what I want you to do tomorrow? When you get here, I want you to pick the spinach, cucumbers, tomatoes, and then, I want twenty pints of strawberries. Once you get them picked, I want you to bring them to the stand. I'll leave the keys in my truck so you can drive them down."

"You got it. I'll see you tomorrow morning." Frankie left with a smile on his face. He really felt like he had done a great job. They'd accomplished a lot. He was enjoying it so much that it didn't seem like work. He pulled into his yard and parked next to the house, not bothering to lock his car. He went inside and began his homework.

* * * * *

Frankie met Isaac at the stand. He could tell immediately that something was wrong. "Frankie, do you think your friends were upset with me yesterday because I made you go back to work?"

"Of course not, why would you think that?" Frankie had a feeling that something else had happened. He followed Isaac back to the field. Before him, he could see a large part of the strawberry crop was destroyed. "Isaac, what happened?"

"I was hoping you could tell me, Frankie."

Frankie had no clue what had happened. "He began to worry that someone was targeting Isaac because of him." He was beginning to live the nightmare all over again. He helped clean up the destroyed area and went to work on the last orders he had been given. He brought the produce down to the stand. Isaac left him in charge, giving him specific instructions for locking everything up. He showed him where to put the money and the key.

"Frankie, I'll see you out here tomorrow morning. I've got to run to Tampa to take a friend to the hospital. I'm trusting you to handle everything. Your lunch is under the stand in a cooler." He slapped Frankie on the back like they were old friends. Then, Frankie watched him drive off.

Jacob drove up and stopped at the stand. "Hey, Jacob, listen, if you are here to talk and goof around, I really can't do that. I'm working."

Jacob shook his head. "No, as much as I miss hanging out with you and Tanya, that is not why I'm here."

"Wait, what do you mean you miss hanging out with Tanya? Did you two have a fight or something?"

Jacob laughed. "No, but for my part in the accident, I'm pretty much grounded for the next three weeks. I'm helping my mom with her rock path and garden. She sent me down to get some strawberries from you. Someone at church said this is the best place to get them. She's going to make her famous strawberry pies. She's even sending one over to your house. I hope she lets me take it so I can see your sister. Tanya didn't tell you I couldn't come over?"

"To tell the truth, I finish work, go home, and start my homework. My mom's been bringing my dinner to my room. After I take my shower, I'm so beat I've been going straight to bed." Frankie kept looking around like he was expecting someone.

"Okay, Frankie, spill it. You expecting a girl or something? You just keep looking around and up and down the road. I mean, if I'm interrupting I can take a hint."

Jacob noticed Frankie didn't smile at his joke. "No, I'm not expecting a girl, but something's going on. After my first day here, someone tore up a bunch of Isaac's spinach plants and left the hoe and my hat next to it. This morning, someone destroyed some of his strawberry plants. Isaac thought maybe one of my friends from school was upset with him because they were goofing around here yesterday, and he made them stop. They damaged some of the produce. What if this is happening because of me?"

"Have you told your parents, Frankie?"

"No, I don't want to worry them, in case there's nothing to it."

"Well, keep your eyes open, and if things keep happening, then, you better watch your back." Jacob paid for his purchases and left. It was a slow day for Frankie. Only two more customers stopped by. At four o'clock, he closed up the stand and stashed the money and the key as he was told.

42

Three weeks had gone by quickly. Isaac's cast was gone, but it was apparent it would take some time for him to get the strength back in it. Frankie was beginning to think that maybe one of his friends had gotten even with Isaac by destroying the strawberries because nothing else had happened for weeks. Frankie finished working and left the farm. He wanted to get home before Jacob picked Tanya up for the prom. Frankie would have liked to have gone, but it was a relief not to meet the prying eyes of all of the teachers and students. Many people still thought Frankie had made up all of the allegations against Mr. Fugate. He knew what had really happened, and nothing could change that.

After dinner, Frankie sat in the living room with his dad, waiting for Tanya. Jacob sat beside him like a nervous little boy. "Man, why are you so nervous? You've stayed with us, you've been dating Tanya all year, so why so nervous?" Frankie laughed when Jacob just shrugged, instead of answering. He actually looked scared.

"She's so beautiful. What if we get there, and everyone else realizes how beautiful she is, and she dumps me?" Both Frankie and his dad laughed.

"Son, if you think she's that shallow, you'd better think again. My girl is crazy for you. But don't let that give you guys any ideas. You're still too young for any kind of major relationship." Mr. Bonita winked at Jacob as he said this.

Frankie's mom entered the room and stopped. She had a gleam in her eyes and a smile from ear to ear. She looked toward the hallway. Tanya stepped out. The rose-colored dress she wore made her skin glow. It was a modest dress with a draped neckline and ended slightly below the knees. It wasn't too formal. Her dark hair had been pulled back from her face and was clipped on each side with the same colored rhinestone barrettes to match her dress. A simple necklace adorned her throat. Tanya looked at Frankie as she touched the necklace he had given her and thanked him. Jacob jumped to his feet and handed her the wrist corsage. The carnations would look beautiful on her dainty wrist. They posed for what felt like a thousand pictures. Finally, Mrs. Bonita allowed them to leave. Jacob was every bit the gentleman. He walked her to the car and held the door. They drove slowly down the drive and turned toward the school. This was going to be a night they would never forget.

Frankie sat in his room, working on his online classes. If he kept at it, he could probably finish all of his school within the next two weeks. He logged into his English class and saw he only had two more papers to write to finish the subject. He had already completed most of the research for them, so why not finish them since he wasn't going anywhere? He felt the old burn returning. It just wasn't fair that he'd missed out on so much this year because of Mr. Fugate. He hadn't heard anything for a long time about the case. Why was it that it took so long to bring a teacher to justice? He began to rub his hands on his thighs. Realizing what was happening, he focused back on the computer screen. He was not going to give in this time.

He hadn't heard Jacob's car pull into the drive. He was just shutting down his computer when Tanya knocked on his door. She poked her head in. "Hey, Frankie. Is everything okay? I saw your light was still on."

"Yeah, sis. I just finished my last online English class. I still have a couple classes in math and science to finish, and then, I'm done. I don't have to work tomorrow, so I figured I'd finish up those two courses. How was the dance?"

Tanya came in and sat on his bed. "It was nice. But it didn't seem the same with you not there. Everyone was talking about Mr.

Fugate. He actually showed up at the dance. He stood there for almost thirty minutes before Mr. Grimhold saw him and had him escorted out. Mr. Fugate was so mad. He kept yelling that it wasn't fair that a student could lie and cost him his career when he was there to help the students. I don't think he's done causing trouble. Be careful, Frankie." She stood up and went to her room.

Frankie thought about what she'd said. He was more concerned about Tanya and Jacob. What if Mr. Fugate was the one responsible for locking them in that cabin? But how would he know about the cabin? Frankie shook the thoughts from his head. He was tired, so he took a shower and went to bed, falling asleep almost immediately.

It seemed like his head had just hit the pillow when he heard the pounding on the door. He looked at his clock. It was almost one o'clock in the morning. Who would be pounding on their door this early? There was a light knock on his door, and then, his dad opened it. "Frankie, I need you to get up and come out here." His dad shut the door without saying another word.

Frankie went to the living room. His parents were sitting across from two officers. What was going on? Frankie sat next to his parents.

"My name is Officer Jared. Could you please tell us where you were this evening?" Frankie looked puzzled but answered quickly.

"I've been here all night. I was working on my online classes."

"Mom, Dad, what's going on?"

Frankie's parents looked at the officers. Officer Jared answered, "Someone vandalized a teacher's house tonight, and he believes it was you."

"Me? Why would he think it was me? I'm taking all of my classes at home now."

Officer Jared looked at his partner. "Mr. Fugate seems to think you have it in for him. Someone threw some bricks through his house windows this evening with messages written on them. He thinks it was you."

Frankie jumped to his feet. "Me?" he screamed. "He thinks I did it?"

His father placed a calming hand on his shoulder. "Frankie, don't say another word. I'll call Mr. Black, and if the officers have any questions, they can go through him." He looked at Officer Jared. "I don't know if you're aware of it, but my son is the reason Mr. Fugate is suspended from school. There's a pending case, so if you have any questions, you need to speak with our lawyer." He handed him Mr. Black's number. "He can fill you in on the details of the case."

Frankie looked completely deflated. When was all of this going to end? He went back to his bed and sat on it. He could hear his parents talking down the hall. From their tone, he knew they were worried. He curled up and went back to sleep.

Morning came quickly. After a quick breakfast with his parents, he headed back to his room to work on his classes. He heard his parents leave for a meeting at the church. He had just started the first class when there was a knock on the door. He looked out the window and saw a police car. When he answered the door, he was face-to-face with Officer Jared.

"Frankie, I need you to come to the station with me. We need to talk. Where are your parents?"

"They're at the church. Can I call them?" Officer Jared gave approval and, then, asked them to call his attorney and meet them at the police station. Frankie did as he was told, then followed the officer to his car. The officer opened the back door for him. Frankie's stomach began to turn flips as he sat in the back seat. At least, he wasn't handcuffed.

Frankie's parents were at the station when he arrived. They had already called Mr. Black, who had left word that Frankie was to say nothing until he came. Frankie followed the officer to a room, sat, and waited. After a few minutes, the door opened, and Sheriff Joseph entered along with Mr. Black.

Sheriff Joseph held out his hand to Frankie. "How you doing, son?"

"Okay, I guess. I'm a little confused as to why I'm here."

"Well, I'm going to explain what is happening. I want you to sit and listen and only answer when your lawyer tells you to. Do you understand?"

"Yes, sir."

Officer Joseph placed a tape recorder in the middle of the table and began. "Frankie, the reason we called you here is that we found some discrepancies in what you told Officer Jared last night. We need to clear some things up. Where were you last night?"

"Like I told Officer Jared, I was at home doing homework. I take all of my classes online now."

The sheriff rubbed his head. "You didn't leave the house and go anywhere?"

Frankie's reply was quick. "No, sir."

The sheriff picked up a remote and pointed it at the television in the corner. "Frankie, we have some surveillance video we would like you to look at." Frankie looked at the screen. It was taken from a convenience store about a mile from his house. He watched as his car pulled in and he got out. He was back out a couple of minutes later with a soda and a bag of donuts.

Sheriff Joseph asked the question again.

Frankie looked at the video and at the sheriff. "I guess I went to the store last night and picked up a snack. I guess I forgot because I stop there almost every day to get a snack. What does this have to do with why I'm here?"

"Did you know that you have to pass Mr. Fugate's house to get to that store?"

"I thought Mr. Fugate lived out near the school, I didn't know he lived anywhere near us. That isn't something that teachers tell their students." He chuckled nervously.

"Just a few more questions. Were you working for Mr. Zook yesterday?"

Frankie thought the change in questions was strange, but he answered it. "Yes, sir, Mr. Zook had to go to Tampa. He asked me to run his stand for him yesterday while he was gone. When I was done, I locked it up and went home."

Another officer came in with a note for the sheriff and waited. "Bring it in, please." The officer came in with a money box and placed it on the table before the sheriff. "Frankie, do you recognize this box?"

Frankie looked at it before he answered. "It looks a lot like the one Mr. Zook has at his stand." The sheriff pulled out some gloves and put them on, then opened the lid. The inside was empty.

"Frankie, Mr. Zook called this morning and told us his money box was missing from the stand. We talked to your parents and got permission to check your car. We found this box under the front passenger seat. Do you know how it got there?"

Frankie could feel the panic beginning to rise. "No, sir, I don't. Just like I told him, I didn't know how the spinach got tore up, or why my hat was found next to the hoe. I also don't know anything about the destroyed strawberries. All I've done is help him. Why is he accusing me?" His voice began to rise in frustration. Mr. Black reached over and patted his hand to calm him down.

The sheriff looked at him. "Mr. Zook didn't say anything about the spinach or strawberries. He didn't accuse you. The only thing he said was that his money box was missing. The officer asked if anyone else had access to it. He gave your name but assured us that you couldn't have taken it. We're just trying to find out what is going on here." He stood and went to the door, speaking to the officer on the other side. The officer came in with a box and set it in front of the sheriff, who began pulling out paper-wrapped bricks. He laid them in front of Frankie. Frankie read the messages. "Prejudiced idiot," "you deserve having your wife leave," "Hispanics rule." Each note was typed and wrapped around a brick. Frankie noticed the sheriff touched them with gloved hands. "These are the bricks we recovered from Mr. Fugate's living room. We know he was at the school for, at least, a half hour because the principal told us he had him escorted out. It's possible that you went to the store, then delivered these bricks through the window."

Frankie sat with his mouth opened. How in the world was he supposed to respond to those accusations? Sheriff Joseph spoke to Frankie. "I don't want you to say anything, Frankie. You are not under arrest. I wanted your side of the story. We'll continue the investigation and let you know when we have something. You're free to leave." The sheriff stood and walked out of the room with all of the evidence.

Frankie looked at Mr. Black. "What just happened? He can't really believe that I threw those bricks through Mr. Fugate's windows or stole the money box, can he?"

Mr. Black stood. "He'll get to the bottom of it. Don't worry. Let's get you back out to your parents." They walked through the station to where his parents were waiting for him.

"Mr. and Mrs. Bonita, I think you should take Frankie home, and I'll meet you there within the hour to discuss this latest event." They nodded and walked out to their car. Frankie felt completely drained.

Mr. Black walked back to the sheriff's office and knocked on his door. The sheriff motioned him in. "Please, tell me that you don't think he's guilty."

Sheriff Joseph rubbed his head. "I don't know what to think. I don't know why Mr. Zook wouldn't tell us about the destroyed produce if he thought Frankie was guilty. He really went to bat for Frankie. He thought maybe his friends were the ones who had destroyed the fruit and maybe stolen the box. They're going to dust it for prints. How's the case coming against Mr. Fugate?" The sheriff and Mr. Black had been friends for years. If his friend thought Frankie was innocent, then, he was probably right.

"We go to court next week, against Mr. Fugate. You know, if you want to get a case thrown out, there is no better way than to discredit the person accusing you." The sheriff nodded. He just couldn't picture Frankie being mean-spirited or violent like this. All of his other teachers, Mr. Zook, and the students painted a different picture of Frankie. Something was wrong. They still had the unsolved kidnapping case. He'd not had time to go over all of that. He thanked Mr. Black and walked him to the door, then turned down the hall to the lab.

Gino was one of the best lab technicians their department had. The sheriff stopped in to see if he had any answers for him.

"Morning, Sheriff," Gino greeted.

"What did you find in all of that mess we brought from the cabin?" Well, inside the bottle of soda, we found a small amount of residue. It turned out to be Xanax. The shirt wrapped around their manacles was actually Frankie's. His name was inside one section. We found a few prints that didn't belong to any of the teens. We haven't run them yet, but we will."

"You got the bricks and the money box, correct? I want them dusted as well. Get back to me as soon as you learn anything."

Gino nodded and went back to work while the sheriff went back to his office.

CHAPTER
43

Frankie was just breaking for an afternoon snack when the phone rang. He heard his mom say they would leave immediately. She called her husband and asked him to meet them at the sheriff's office. "Frankie, that was the sheriff, and he wants us to come in right now." Frankie rolled his eyes and walked with his mom to the car. How much longer was this going to go on?

They pulled up at the sheriff's department at the same time Tanya and Jacob arrived, followed by the Wingates. As Frankie turned toward the door, he saw Isaac Zook pull up. "Why do you think he's here?" His mom shrugged.

They walked in as a united group. There was power in numbers. Once inside, they were taken to a large room and asked to wait. When the door closed. Jacob's father prayed over them. Since none of them knew why they were there, it would be good to pray for God's protection on them. They waited for almost an hour before the sheriff came in, carrying a box. He set it on the table.

"Recognize this?" he asked as he held up several strips of fabric. Frankie recognized the school logo.

"Hey, that's my PE shirt. Where'd you find it?" He watched as the officer pulled out a bottle of Xanax. "What are you doing with those? I threw them away in the woods."

He sat down and looked at all of them. "From what we've been able to piece together, Mr. Fugate was furious at Frankie. He blames

Frankie for his suspension, and he's been following you, Frankie. He was responsible for your damaged tires and the scratches in your car. You really need to start locking your car. That's how he got your hat to lay beside the hoe. We found his fingerprints on both of them. His prints were on the paper wrapped around the bricks. That was to be expected. They matched the missing blocks from the back of his house. He wanted to make us think you were mad at him and did this. He'd been watching you at the farm and saw you put the money box away and hide the key. He took the box and removed the money and placed it in your car." The sheriff boxed everything back up and stood.

"He's also responsible for Jacob and Tanya being locked up in the cabin. He hadn't planned on trying to kill them. He found your bottle of pills and drugged the soda. That's why you fell asleep and didn't remember anything. You had no idea he was watching you or doing this, did you?"

Frankie looked horrified. "Why would he do this? I've never given him a reason."

The sheriff ran his hand through his hair. "I know you're aware his wife ran off with a Mexican. Well, they were killed in a car crash. He just broke. He thought his wife would come back to him at some point. He blamed all Hispanics. He started taking his frustration out on the Hispanic kids at school. The others said nothing because they were afraid. You were the only one to challenge him. He couldn't handle you standing up to him, so he decided to make you go away. I want you to know you've been cleared of everything, and you're free to go."

Mr. Bonita stood with his family. "What's going to happen to him—Mr. Fugate, I mean?"

"He'll be charged for his crimes, and then, it's up to the courts to decide his fate."

Mr. Bonita smiled. "Well, I'm glad that he'll get what is coming to him. He needs to be punished for what he did." Frankie looked at his dad and, then, looked away. Once again, his thoughts were in conflict.

Frankie arrived at work and started before Isaac had come out of the house. He worked hard. Isaac sat on the porch and watched

Frankie. Each swing of the hoe sent dirt flying. There was anger behind each swing, and Isaac didn't know why. He went to his truck and noticed Frankie had already loaded the produce for the stand.

At noon, Frankie joined Isaac at the stand for lunch. Isaac handed him a bottle of iced tea and a sandwich. He watched Frankie eat in silence. "What has you so bothered that you were killing the dirt out there, and now you eat in silence?"

Frankie looked down to the ground. "We found who tore up your crops and stole your money box. It was Mr. Fugate. He was trying to blame me. He's the one who left my sister and best friend in that cabin."

Isaac listened carefully. "So why does this seem to bother you so much? I thought you would be happy he was finally caught."

"It's not that, Isaac. I don't know. I keep thinking about what I did to you and how you forgave me. I guess I feel sorry for Mr. Fugate. I don't understand why he did what he did. They said it's because he lost it after his wife ran off, then died. But I think about all of the mean things he did to my family and me. How can I forgive that? Haven't I done enough already? I shouldn't have to forgive him."

"Ahhh, but that's where you're wrong, Frankie. Do you remember when Peter asked Jesus how many times he had to forgive someone? What was his answer?"

"He said we should forgive seventy times seven. Does that mean that I have to forgive him for everything he did?"

"If you don't, it will cause a break in your relationship with God. I am not telling you this is easy because it isn't. When you first hit me and drove off, I was angry. I was upset you didn't stop, I was mad I couldn't work, I was angry that God allowed this to happen. From what you've been telling me, maybe God allowed this to happen to teach all of you to forgive."

Frankie nodded his head. "I read an article several years ago about a lady whose little girl was murdered. The mother and all of her family went to visit the man in prison. He had been a family friend. They sat and talked with him and told him that they forgave him for what he'd done. They prayed with him. I used to wonder how they could do that. There had to be so much pain."

"I'm sure there was, Frankie. It's a pain that will never completely go away. But by forgiving him, they could move on with their own lives. They put his life on God's hands. I'll pray that God will give you the strength to do what you know you need to do."

Frankie thanked him and went back to work. When he got home that night, he was quiet at the table. His dad looked concerned. "Did everything go all right at work today?"

Frankie just nodded. "Dad, will you go with me to see Mr. Fugate at the jail?"

Frankie's mom looked concerned. "Frankie, I don't think that is such a good idea. Why would you want to do such a thing?"

Frankie laid down his fork. "Today, at lunch, Isaac and I were talking about forgiveness. I don't like what he did to our family or me, but I have to let him know I forgive him. I also need to let you know that I forgive you, Dad. You were trying to do what you thought was best for me, and things just got messed up." When he looked up, he could see tears in his dad's eyes.

"When did you become such a man? I am so sorry for what I put all of you through. Yes, Frankie, I'll go with you to the jail." They continued eating in silence.

Frankie's dad called the sheriff to get permission to visit Mr. Fugate. Mr. Fugate didn't want to see Frankie or his family. Frankie tried several more times and finally gave up. Mr. Fugate's trial lasted only two weeks. There was so much evidence against Mr. Fugate that he pleaded guilty. He sat in the courtroom, staring straight ahead. He was charged with false imprisonment. The judge set aside time for the family to speak to the court before sentencing. Frankie and his family prayed for the right words.

The day of sentencing, Frankie walked into the courtroom, his stomach full of butterflies. When he was called to the podium, he walked confidently forward. Mr. Fugate looked down at the table. "Your honor, I would like to say that this man here has made life really difficult for my family and me, as well as many others. The memories of some of the things he did, the humiliation I felt in school, the fear I felt when my sister and best friend were missing will stay with me for a long time. However, when I look at this man here, I see someone who never learned to forgive. If he had forgiven his wife and himself, maybe he would not have gone down that destructive path. Mr. Fugate, I am here today, speaking on behalf of my entire family and the Wingate family. We want you to know that we forgive you. We hold no grudge toward you. We are hoping that one day you may reach out to us, and we'll be able to talk. Your honor, this man has gone through as much pain as what he put us through. I am asking, your honor, that when you make your ruling, you will rule justly and with leniency because, your honor, that is what forgiveness is all about. Thank you."

Frankie returned to his seat. The judge asked if there was anyone else who wanted to speak. The courtroom was silent.

The judge began to shuffle around his papers. "Will the defendant please rise. Mr. Fugate, what you have done to these two families is reprehensible. You set out to destroy a young man because of your prejudices. You held two young people against their will and almost cost them their lives. You destroyed the property of others to try to frame this young man. The penalty could get you five years in prison, and I personally think you deserve that and more. However, I always take into consideration what the family has to say. It is quite evident that this young man has truly forgiven you. I will take into consideration what he has said. I pray that one day you may learn to forgive yourself because that is where this really must begin. Having said that, I am sentencing you to two years in prison. You will be fined ten thousand dollars for the destruction of Mr. Zook's property and Frankie's car. I do hope that you spend that time thinking about what this young man said here. The court is adjourned." He slammed his gavel on the desk.

Mr. Fugate turned and looked at Frankie. The hatred that was once in his eyes was gone, replaced by bewilderment. "Why? After all I did, why would you choose to forgive me?"

Frankie walked toward him. "Because, Mr. Fugate, that is what God tells me I must do. I meant what I said. I hope that one day you will allow me to sit and talk with you. Maybe you and my family can get to know each other and be friends." Frankie held out his hand.

Mr. Fugate looked at him and grabbed him in a hug. "I truly am sorry for what I've done. Please forgive me."

Frankie slapped him on the back.

"I forgive you." He watched as the officers put handcuffs on him and led him from the room. Tears began to form in his eyes. His parents came up and put their arms around him.

"Frankie, we are so proud of you," his mom said with a smile. They turned and walked out of the room.

The end.

ABOUT THE AUTHOR

Sandra Stiles is a middle school teacher. She lives in Sarasota, Florida, with her husband. She was inspired to write books by one of her students. After having students write a story and modeling one for them, it was suggested she write books to put on her shelf that students would want to read. When she isn't writing stories and poetry or encouraging her students to write, you can find her reading and writing reviews for her blog. In her spare time, she likes to quilt and paint. Much of her inspiration comes from nature.

CPSIA information can be obtained
at www.ICGtesting.com
Printed in the USA
BVHW081538050321
601818BV00001B/178